A
CHANGE
OF SCENE

By the same author

HOUSE OF GOLD

THE TIME OF ADAM

YELLOW ROSES

Elizabeth Cullinan

A
CHANGE
OF SCENE

W · W · *Norton & Company* · *New York* · *London*

The author gratefully acknowledges grants received from the National Endowment for the Arts and from the Carnegie Fund.

The text of this book is composed in V.I.P. Palatino, with display type set in typositor Carolus Roman and Carpenter. Composition and manufacturing are by the Maple Vail Book Manufacturing Group. Book and binding design by Antonina Krass.

Library of Congress Cataloging in Publication Data
Cullinan, Elizabeth, 1933–
A change of scene.

I. Title.
PS3553.U32C5   1982   813'.54   81–18875
AACR2

W. W. Norton & Company, Inc. 500 Fifth Avenue, New York, N.Y. 10110
W. W. Norton & Company Ltd. 37 Great Russell Street, London WC1B 3NU

1 2 3 4 5 6 7 8 9 0

ISBN 0-393-01568-8

For Margaret Cullinan

A
CHANGE
OF SCENE

One I used to try not to lose my temper, for fear of saying something that would haunt me. But how much likelier it is that our ugly and for that matter our pretty speech and behavior will instead lose their sharpness. I've learned to appreciate the occasional stab of regret, the pangs of past joys, and recently I had some of both, brought on by a telephone call from Tomás O'Domhnaill whom I knew when I lived in Ireland some years ago. I missed the call; I'd stepped out of the office, but Tomás left word that he could be reached at the Abbey Victoria Hotel. The girl who took the message misspelled my name as usual—putting the "e" on Ann, leaving it off Clarke—and I was irritated both with her and unreasonably with him as I reached for the phone book to look up the address of the Abbey Victoria. It turned out to be a few blocks from the television station where I work. I was startled to think of Tomás so close by—that he should be in New York was amazing enough. I thought it unlikely that he'd had the desire or the money for an American vacation, and I decided he was over on business, though I was at a loss when it came to devising specific business in the United States for the Cork correspondent of a Dublin newspaper. Whatever his purpose here it was inevitable that he should have hit on a hotel that had, for at least part of its name, the word Abbey with its connotations of his country's literary past glory. "Christened no doubt by Yeats himself," I imagined him saying to his friends, as they sat over their pints of stout.

The Abbey Victoria would thus have been chosen in the spirit of perversity and pride, innocence and shrewdness that I thought of for so long as Irish, though now I sometimes wonder whether that frame of mind might have been peculiar to Tomás and his friends. In any case it was he who plunged me into Irish life as I knew it best. This was not long after we were introduced through the good or at least well-meaning offices of Neil Driscoll, an Irish journalist I met over here when I was a production assistant at the station. I was happy with that job, which was my first, and three years went by before I felt the need to move on, but there were no openings at the station, and unlike most of my friends I wasn't about to move into marriage. I was in love, but the man was already married, unsatisfactorily but firmly, or so it seemed to me, for I'm Catholic, though this man made me question what I'd previously taken for granted about religion and everything else—leaving me emotionally stranded in the process.

The times we now live in may better serve someone at that desolate juncture—there are protest politics, and Eastern religion, and health clubs to help drown out and work off your sorrows; but fifteen or so years back people hadn't yet learned to deal with life on those fierce terms. At least I hadn't, and looking to an earlier and even gentler time I sent myself on an ocean voyage to Europe, to Ireland, and for an extended stay. Why Ireland? I'd once had a vacation in Europe and of my two favorite places, Amsterdam and Dublin, Dublin was cheaper. Besides, I had an image of myself steadily refining the raw materials of an unfamiliar daily life, reducing them to a kind of certitude that I felt would make me more interesting and less vulnerable to people, and I believed that for this I needed to eavesdrop without worrying about vocabulary or irregular verbs. At the back of my mind there was also the idea that living in a chronically Catholic country would automatically sort out my feelings on that whole subject.

The producer I worked for then was interested in doing something on the Common Market, and Neil Driscoll was one of the consultants to the proposed series. Neil was assigned to the U.N. and married to a hearty American girl named Beatrice who was twenty years younger than he, wore her hair in a braid, and spoke with an Irish accent. A month before I left, she telephoned and said, "You're coming to us for lunch. How about next Wednesday?"

They lived on Second Avenue in a big, modern apartment that Beatrice had countrified with a lot of Irish tweed and earthenware, but four-year-old Tricia Driscoll was a streamlined little girl with her sleek pageboy and denim dress. All during lunch she kept lifting her skirt to show that she wasn't wearing underpants, which embarrassed her father. Neil was a shy man, and Beatrice did all the talking. "Whereabouts in Dublin do you plan to live?" she asked me.

I said, "I thought I'd look for a place in Merrion Square."

"Lots of atmosphere but no comfort," Beatrice said. "Try the Mespil Flats where Neil and I spend the winter. They're at least liveable though not by our standards, God knows." Beatrice came from Grosse Pointe, and I reminded myself that her standards weren't necessarily mine. "Where will you go when you first get to Dublin?" she asked, and I told her the Shelbourne.

"The Shelbourne," said Neil, "is full of English gentry on holiday. They post arrivals on a slate in the lobby!"

"We could try and get Oona to put you up. That's Oona Ross the novelist," Beatrice told me.

One of Oona Ross's books had been made into a movie that I'd seen three or four times. I could even put a face to the name, for when the movie was released there'd been a newspaper interview with the writer. She was a widow, according to the article; in the photograph she and her three daughters were leaning against a small dilapidated car and they had their arms around each other's shoulders.

"She's liable to forget, so take down her address. Addresses," Beatrice corrected herself. "There's one in the country and one in Dublin. Will you be buying any clothes?" I mentioned something about a winter coat, and she said, "Go to Plura Belle. They'll make up something that'll cost less than a nice coat at Saks. Dublin hairdressers are cheap, too, and the bookshops are wonderful, especially Greene's. If you need a doctor, call Brian Mayne. I hope you're getting all this down." She pointed to the piece of paper she'd given me. "Take my advice, treat yourself to a pair of earrings at Louis Wine's. It's an investment."

Left to myself I doubt that I'd have followed through on Beatrice's next idea—that I change my Cork hotel reservation—but at that point Neil took over; Cork was his birthplace. He said, "We'll have Josie Flood cancel for you and book you in at the Metropole."

"Josie was Neil's first love." Beatrice made a face. "Even so I adore her, and you will, too. You're bound to love everyone in Cork."

But friendship isn't automatically transferable. Anyway I wanted to get to know people who were at my stage of life and seemed to be going in my direction, and for this reason I'd applied to Trinity College Dublin. Neil disapproved. "You'd be better off at U.C.D. among your own kind," he said.

My Irish name brought me no treasury of Gaelic custom and Celtic lore. My mother looked down on that sort of thing, and my father had no interest in it. When for the first time I rode through the amber mountainscapes, the gray villages, the mile after mile of green fields haphazardly parted by broken walls of unmortared stone, all this stern beauty had come as a complete surprise, but Neil's remark made me realize that further investigation might reveal something all too familiar in those mountains and villages, and I began to have misgivings, for I had no desire to be strictly speaking among my own. My reasons for going in the first place had something to do with getting away from them and their troubles—none of it original, for all families follow the same plan, pursue the same dream, and when families fail, it often comes down to a failure to put the dream to some good use. At least that's the trouble with my family. All his life my father has been a gambler, convinced that some day he'd win a fortune, but I don't think he has any idea what he'd do with a lot of money. The attempt to get it has consumed his energy and left him without resources. My mother's great desire in life is prestige, though she thinks of it as holiness, since the company she aspires to consists mainly of priests and nuns and their relatives. In this parochial society it doesn't seem to matter that she wants too much from people, or the wrong thing—admiration instead of companionship.

My parents' dreams resulted in lives of bitterness for them and a heritage of insecurity for me and my sister, Barbara, but there's more to love than happiness. I wasn't particularly glad the day I sailed away from the three of them, and the Irish contingent on board—all either timid or rowdy—didn't help. I took up with a fellow from Connecticut who was in his last year of medicine at Queens University in Belfast. Together we explored the rest of the ship, dancing at night to the first-class band which was five pieces instead of three, crashing the superior cabin-class tea, and in between expeditions playing cards or dozing in our own deckchairs. One morning we were sunbathing. Nearby were three middle-aged Irish bachelors shouting together over a game of shuffleboard and singing pop songs at the top of their lungs. I said to my medical student friend, "I think I've made a mistake going to Ireland," and I drew his attention to the shuffleboard court.

"They're not typical," he said. "They've been living in the States too long."

This was Tuesday. At midnight on Thursday when the ship dropped anchor in Cobh harbor, you could make out a dark shape in the near distance, like another hull in silent communion with ours. It wasn't a particularly inspiring sight, but the next morning under a watery lavender sky the long green hump of land looked immensely inviting— placid and picturesque, like an enormous garden. Well, I said to myself, we'll see.

Two Pure use unsoftened by individual habit and unsweetened by private possession, plus the attempt to disguise this, deadens hotel atmosphere, but at the Cork Metropole human nature had managed to prevail. Signs of hard wear were in plain view there, speaking warmly of all the feet that got to know their way around those carpeted corridors; of bodies that claimed the overstuffed armchairs in the lobby and were revived by cups of tea, or whiskeys; of keys familiarly collected or relinquished at the mahogany reception desk, under the amiable supervision of a line of elderly clerks like the one who had me sign in. "Mrs. Flood's waiting for you in the lounge," he said, "God love her. You've a letter as well, Miss Clarke." I put the envelope in my handbag, considered stopping off first at my room, and did instead what I decided was the right thing.

It wasn't quite noon but half the tables in the lounge were occupied by men in business suits having drinks and quietly arguing. The lone woman was small, strikingly plain, and in spite of a seaman's knit cap pulled down around her ears, obviously dressed up in the navy blue suit under her raincoat. I went over, and she said, "You're the American so you've got to be Ann, and I suppose I must be Josie."

This astringent speech gave me a feeling of being somehow in the wrong. But not entirely, I told myself and asked, "Was this a lot of trouble? Neil insisted."

"Darling Neil," said Josie, "we were engaged once," and she proceeded to tell me the whole sad story. Any response seemed tactless, and I ended up asking if I could give her lunch. "Thanks very much but I must get back to the shop. I'm a stationer." She said this with a dedicated air that was devoid of censure, though it set me straight; I moved to the edge of my chair. "Not to worry," Josie said, "my assistant's holding the fort. What time this evening would suit you? You're to meet Owen and Sheila O'Reilly— Beatrice's orders. Let's make it half eight here at the Metropole in the bar. Then maybe on Sunday you'll come out driving with Seamus and me." She got to her feet. "Cheerio, Ann." And tugging her knit cap over her ears, Josie went off.

I was in the mood for a sandwich but when I was seated in the dining room I found out I'd come to the wrong place. "You'd want to go to the lounge for your sandwiches," the waiter told me. "There's nothing but dinners here." I ordered sole amandine, which came with exactly seven bits of almond. "Come to look up your kin, Yank?" asked the waiter as he laid the plate in front of me.

"I haven't any family in Ireland," I said. "Not that I know of." But blood isn't the only kind of kinship—a truth that was brought home to me later in the afternoon as I walked the narrow streets of Cork. The attached houses gave a heartening impression of poverty and security, deprivation and comfort. Butcher shops abounded, and betting parlors were only somewhat fewer. (The origin of my father's troubles?) I liked the humble little shops called Draper's though I couldn't believe anyone would want the plain blouses and slips or the sleazy scarves on display. It would rain for five minutes; then for another five minutes there'd be both sun and rain; then the rain would stop, and the sun go in, as the sky gathered itself into a mass of low, slate-blue clouds. The air was cool but sultry and it made me drowsy. I went back to the Metropole and fell asleep; when I woke it was dark out, and my watch had stopped. I reached up and turned on the radio. A man was talking in a foreign language; then fiddle music suddenly came reeling out. I drew the curtains and sat down to read my letter, which was from my sister.

Dearest Ann,

Hope you've forgotten all my embarrassing tears at the pier. It was just that I'd begun missing you. How much I still do, you can probably imagine. Anyway, I must get this off, so you'll have it when you arrive in case you're homesick. Don't be. Just be sure that at the end of the year you *come* home. . . .

Barbara is two years older than I, and the habit of minding me, which she hated when we were young, is ingrained in her, even though I grew up to be temperamentally the elder, which makes her concern burdensome to me now, impairing my life in some way that has to do with the importance of getting things straight. I put her letter aside and went into the bathroom and washed my face and brushed my hair. I decided to go to the lounge for a sandwich, but when I got there what looked like the same men who'd been drinking and arguing at lunchtime were back, only more of them. Every table was occupied, so I went to the dining room and had another dinner.

I like bars—the dissipation in the atmosphere and equally the order in the dissipation: those regiments of bottles and glasses, coasters and stirrers; the little tables in formation. Though I drink very little I like drinks—the smell, the kick, the deliciousness; then I like sitting back and sizing up the seductions, the quarrels, and the con games fostered by that twilit atmosphere of lowered inhibitions and heightened sensation.

Attractions of a different sort were available at the Metropole bar—a brightly lit place full of noise. The lineup of bottles was meager, the air smelled simply and powerfully of beer, and like the crowd in the lounge everyone seemed to be arguing, but these voices were raised. Owen O'Reilly blended right in there, though his large head of tangled gray-gold ringlets, and the toothsized gaps in his smile would anyplace else have made him as striking as Josie Flood. "What will you drink?" he said to me, and I asked for Scotch; then I noticed that everyone else was drinking stout, and when Owen returned from the bar he said, "Here's your expensive foreign stuff."

"Expensive compared to Irish," his wife Sheila explained. She was beautifully softspoken though she spoke hardly at all that evening; then just before closing time she leaned over to me and said, "You'd better come to us tomorrow. Owen'll call for you here. You'll come for lunch."

I had no umbrella and the next day I held my raincoat over my head as I dodged after Owen through one winding street after another. I might have been a captive taken on a deliberately roundabout route, impossible to retrace, but were this the plan, I'd have outwitted it. In my mind I often return to that interesting house, one of an isolated row of three or four, all Georgian, narrow and plain like bony old aristocrats. The O'Reillys' drawing room had very little furniture and no curtains. The windows were open, and rain was blowing in, but no one paid any attention. They had two children, a quiet smart little girl of nine named Nuala, and Sean who was a year old and trying to talk, chirping desperately like a captured bird. Sheila said, "Someone else is coming, but we won't wait. He's habitually late."

We were downstairs in the dining room when Tomás O'Domhnaill dashed in, patting his wiry black hair, trying to subdue it. "Sorry Sheila, but I very nearly missed my deadline," he said as he sat down.

"Tomás works for *The Irish Press*," Sheila told me and turning to him she said, "Ann is from New York."

Tomás and I looked at each other across the table. There was something turn-of-the-century about his appearance —the small moustache, or the cut of his suit, or his haircut —but I decided rather cooly that he was attractive of his kind, and his blue eyes registered some such cool appraisal of me but nothing more, no spark of desire, and I immediately lost interest in him.

Sheila said, "I hope you like lamb stew, Ann."

It was a refined version we ate that day. The lamb

consisted of chops, and the potatoes were passed separately. As I gave myself one, Owen said, "A Clarke with a single pratie?"

Tomás turned to me and said, "Irish descent, are you?"

"Yes, but not very," I said, and he turned away.

"I'm after meeting Paddy Quigley outside the *Press*," he said.

Sheila gave him a longsuffering look. "Must you use that expression? I'm sure Ann agrees it's a vulgarism."

I said, "Which expression?"

" 'After having,' " said Tomás, "is derived from the Irish," and he reeled off a sentence in the choppy language I'd heard on the radio in the Metropole.

Sheila said, "Tomás is a native speaker."

"I was born in the *Gaeltacht*," he informed me.

"A part of Ireland where Irish is the native language," Sheila explained. "Tomás is from Donegal."

"Oh," I said, "I was thinking of going there. I'd like to see the Aran Islands." Tomás looked thunderstruck. I asked, "Aren't they across the bay?"

It was as if you were to tell some New Englanders that you believed Martha's Vineyard to lie off the pristine coast of Maine. Owen burst out laughing, but Tomás was disgusted. "You're thinking of Galway!"

Sheila said, "Donegal is the place to go if you're interested in Irish culture."

"Forget about Aran," said Tomás. He was above all else blunt. "So we're in the same line of work," he said to me a little later. I gave him a blank look, and he asked, "Aren't the press and the television what you people call 'media?' "

I said, "I don't call them that."

After lunch the company increased by two, a couple of friends of Tomás's who came by with a half dozen bottles of stout. Sheila put on a record of a man singing without accompaniment—a kind of *belcanto* version of the reeling music I'd heard on the radio. I understood that I was supposed to think this music wonderful, but it sounded erratic to me. From time to time Tomás and his friends spoke to each other in low voices. One of them was a poet who wrote only in Irish, but I never learned which of the two this was, for they didn't talk to me, though at one point I realized they were talking about me. I caught something that sounded like Driscoll; then I heard the plain English "television." I thought they should have put off discussing me till I wasn't around, and later when Tomás asked, "What brings you to Ireland, Ann?" I gave him a smart answer.

"I have to buy a coat."

He turned back to his friends and said something, and they all smiled. They were beginning to spoil things for me, and I sat forward and said, "I ought to be going."

"Tomás will see you to the Metropole," Sheila said.

He drove at breakneck speed and with deadly concentration, getting us back to the hotel in no time. "*Slán leat,* Ann," he said as I left the car, a classic Volkswagen that looked as if it had been driven hard.

By comparison, Seamus Flood's boxy little Hillman looked brand new, but both car and Seamus went briefly out of commission that Sunday when we were caught in torrential rain on the Old Head of Kinsale. "Let me have one of my tablets, Jo," he said. He seemed remarkably calm; so did Josie.

She found the tablets in his coat pocket and put them in his hand, saying, "You're not bad at all, love." A couple of minutes dragged by; then Seamus sighed, got the car started, and drove us on into the town of Kinsale for tea.

It was eight o'clock by the time Seamus and Josie dropped me off at the Metropole, where the desk clerk greeted me with a long wink. "Someone's waiting for you in the lounge," he said.

It was Tomás O'Domhnaill, sitting at a table near the door, looking rather pleased with himself. I joined him, and he said, "Will we have a drink?"

Something about him made me want to do the wrong

thing or at least the thing I felt would be wrong to his way of thinking. He was so ready to disapprove, and it was so easy to gratify him. I crossed my legs and said, "All right, I'll have a Scotch."

He looked up at the ceiling. "The problem is this," he said, "it's after hours."

"Well then I won't have anything."

Tomás smiled and frowned at the same time. "We can have drinks right enough, if you'll order. As a *bona fide* traveler you're free to drink after hours."

It occurred to me that he'd simply stopped by to get a drink; then it occurred to me that he could have bought some stout and gone, as his friends had the day before, to someone's house. "All right, let's have a drink," I said.

"That's the girl." He signaled for a waiter, and a young boy in badly fitting, worn and shiny tails came over and took the order.

I sat back and said, "That sounds like an easy law to get around."

"Simplicity itself," said Tomás, "like most laws, and meant to be broken." The boy brought our drinks. Tomás paid, lifted his glass and reduced the level of stout by two full inches, lowered the glass, wiped his moustache and said, "When are you off to Dublin?"

"Tomorrow morning on the nine o'clock train." I wondered if he were planning to see me off and decided that was unlikely.

"You must be in a great hurry to leave Cork."

"I might as well get where I'm going."

"And where will you go when you get there?" he asked. I thought I knew more or less how he'd react to the Shelbourne, and he didn't disappoint me: "No doubt that was Neil Driscoll's idea," he said, and I didn't bother to correct him. "I sometimes get up to Dublin," he said. "I stay at a guesthouse where they give you bed and breakfast for a few shillings."

"But is your name posted on a blackboard in the lobby?"

"You could probably have it in lights over the front door with your dollars!" He roared laughing at this; then he asked, "Where will you go when you leave the Shelbourne?" I told him what I had in mind, and he said, "Merrion Square's very dear. A flat there might cost four or five pounds a week."

Four pounds was at that time about twelve dollars, but I didn't let on how far below my most optimistic estimates this figure was. "What would you suggest?" I asked.

"Read the ads." Tomás reached into his coat pocket for a newspaper and handed it to me. "Compliments of the staff." I scanned the front page: a prize dog had been run over on the main street of a place called Dundalk; in County Monaghan a man had murdered his sister by hitting her over the head with a spade; an Italian Festival was being promoted in the shops of Dublin; a campaign was under way to remove the English destination signs from the buses and replace them with signs written in Irish.

I folded the newspaper and said, "Is Irish a difficult language?"

"Are you thinking of learning Irish?" he asked with raised eyebrows.

"I might." On the strength of this Tomás suggested another drink, but I said, "Not for me." He called the waiter, and I ordered the pint of stout. When it was brought and paid for, I stood up and said, "Well, I've got to get up early tomorrow." I'm likelier to sit things out to the bitter end than to quit while I'm ahead, but it had occurred to me that I was wasting time with Tomás, pursuing something that had only a limited future, if that. And besides, weren't any number of such encounters ahead of me in Ireland? But up in my room I felt a little let down. I began to wonder whether I'd made a mistake, choosing ahead of time to settle in Dublin, whether I should have arranged to investigate life in Cork—or Limerick, or Galway, or some other little Irish city.

I slept badly that night and the next morning I felt disgruntled, speeding across the country. The train was an express to Dublin, and I shared a compartment with a family—soft, tidy, fairhaired mother; bleary-eyed father; and three children, two girls with black curls and a boy whose straight bright red hair was plastered down with water. They were quiet children, but when the train got moving, they let themselves go and began to sing. "Ireland, Boys, Hurrah," "Young Roddy McCorley," "Wrap the Green Flag Round Me," "Brennan on the Moor"—it was a rousing repertoire, but the song they fell back on again and again was "The Bells of Shandon," a ballad that struck a melancholy chord in me with the lines:

> . . . On this I ponder, where'er I wander,
> And thus grow fonder, Sweet Cork, of thee . . .

Those were my sentiments.

Three Four names were chalked on the Shelbourne blackboard: Lord Lansdowne, Mrs. Fitzmaurice, Mr. Graham-Jones, Mr. Carr. I read them through twice before going over to the reception desk, where a young woman dressed in black consulted the register and then informed me that there'd been some slipup. "You're booked for tomorrow, the nineteenth, Miss Clarke. We'll have to put you someplace else for the time being." She tucked a loose strand of her beautiful auburn hair back into its becomingly unfashionable roll. "You can wait in the lounge."

Not so fast, I silently told her. "Have I any mail?" Two letters were waiting for me. "Thank you," I said and took myself off to the big room full of easy chairs where people sat drinking coffee and reading newspapers or mail. A woman with an English accent was talking loudly and at a great rate; then a small boy in uniform drifted by, paging someone in a disembodied sort of voice that made the name sound like a bar of plainsong.

One of my letters bore an astonishing script that looked as if the hand holding the pen had suddenly got shoved across the envelope; engraved on the back was the country address Neil and Beatrice had given me for Oona Ross. The other letter was from my mother—three pages, back and front, of her large, legible backhand, heavily underlined, and punctuated at such a pitch of emotion that after a few lines I had to raise my eyes to the window.

One way or another the men passing the hotel reminded me of Tomás O'Domhnaill—they had that wiry hair, or their clothes didn't fit right, or they seemed vaguely belligerent. As for the girls, they all looked healthy and pretty. It came over me that I was probably further in spirit from them than I was from the people in the Shelbourne lounge, and by way of taking steps to correct this, I tore open my other letter. Inside the envelope was a second envelope where the message was scrawled:

> Do ring us at *An Uaimh* (trunk call—say Ah Noom) 37043.
> If no answer ring 764326 in Dublin.
>
> > In haste,
> >
> > O. Ross

It took me several minutes to decipher this. When I did I realized that one of the little pages was walking through the lounge chanting my name. I got up and went back to the desk, where the auburn-haired woman said, "You're room's ready," and she handed me the key. "I think you'll be comfortable there."

It was a beautiful room with a view of Stephen's Green, but I quickly tired of having people come to vacuum, rearranging my possessions; however three days of searching the ads in *The Irish Press* turned up no flats in Merrion Square. The couple of possibilities elsewhere were blandly adequate, and I turned them both down. My notion of living abroad had a lot to do with a certain seamy coziness that I associated with the word "lodgings," located in my mind on a street that had seen better days, and peopled with raffish characters, chivied and cheated by a sly landlady who, herself, had seen better days. I didn't seriously believe that any such place would be feasible, but by the end of the week I'd found a flat that actually met my screwy specifications. I'd also bought a coat and I had Beatrice to thank for both. I'd stuck to her list—eating at Bewley's, browsing at Greene's, getting my hair washed by Paul of Ann Street, and buying myself a coat at Plura Belle, a cubbyhole lined with shelves full of tweed and sweaters. A woman beautifully dressed from these shelves led me to a rack containing four coats, all well cut and obviously too large for me, but as I tried each one, she held it at the shoulders or the back. I said I thought the Chesterfield suited me, and she walked me over to the tweed, where I reached for a pale, heathery blue. "That'd be horridly impractical," she said. "Though American winters aren't as messy as ours."

I said, "I'm spending the winter in Dublin."

She got down some brown material that had a fleck of green running through it. "There," she said, draping it across my chest. It felt like a carpet.

I said, "With my coloring?" My hair is dark brown, and I have brown eyes.

"You want to underscore it," she said, and the idea appealed to me. Where in Ireland could I do better? I asked myself and settled on a Chesterfield in the brown. She got out her tapemeasure and said, "Are you a student?" and I said I was. "Fixed up with a place to live?"

"Not yet," I said, and she straightened.

"A friend of mine by the name of Stella Philbin has one or two flats in her house. She's a charming person, a widow."

I felt I had to ask, "Whereabouts is the house?"

"Fitzwilliam Square," she said. "Let me ring Stella and you can go round there this afternoon."

Though I doubted that this fashionable woman's friend could offer the slightly seedy atmosphere I had in mind, the prospect of seeing another flat cheered me, and crossing Dawson Street on my way back to the Shelbourne, I turned for a good look at the source of this luck. That was when I noticed the name Plura Belle above the shopwindow. It seemed to sanction the step I'd taken, and I had the satisfying feeling that I was acting according to plan.

Fitzwilliam Square has a definite air of grandeur, but it's comfortable grandeur. There's something reassuring about those identically proportioned Georgian houses facing each other across their pretty park. Stella Philbin's stood out by virtue of a luxuriant Virginia creeper that the first days of autumn had turned red and brown. The door was a smart khaki, and there were four brass bells, but only one with a nameplate—Mr. Hughes, it said, and rather than pick a completely dark horse I rang his bell. A tall blond girl in a lab coat answered the door, and I asked to see Mrs. Philbin. "You've got the wrong bell," she said, "but do come in." The entrance hall was the size of a fairly large room. From behind a door to the right came the sound of a dentist's drill; ahead was a staircase with a spacious landing where a gray angora cat sat washing itself. "I'll go get the maid," said the blond girl and she ran down the hall to a door under the stairs, calling, "Theresa!" Somewhere close by a telephone rang, and the girl came back apologizing, "That's mine." As she started upstairs, the cat took off.

Five minutes later Theresa appeared, wiping her hands on her apron. She was a kind of parody of Irish beauty: tightly curled, pitch black hair; blue eyes with a cast in the left and in the right an expression of curiosity and dread; a high, unhealthy color in her cheeks. That day and every day I ever saw her, she wore a dark crepe dress, a flowered apron, and lowheeled black suede pumps with white ankle socks. She was smoking a cigarette. I told her I was there to see the room, and she nodded. "Madam said I was to show it to you."

The landing where the cat had been sitting led to something like a minor wing of the house. Here behind a huge desk was the blond girl still on the telephone. We went past her to a square of corridor with a door at the back, which Theresa opened, saying, "It's what we call the return room, or the box room." I was pleasantly surprised. The walls were white, papered rather than painted, and there was a lot of furniture, all of it small, white, and wicker except for the wardrobe in the corner and the daybed which was covered by a sophisticated sweep of gray velveteen. Theresa patted a low cabinet and said, "Here's your food safe."

I asked, "What about a stove?"

"I believe Madam has something in mind," said Theresa. "There's your hot water." She pointed to an apparatus attached to the washbasin. "The meter's just outside." She brought me back to the corridor and showed me how to work the metal box on the floor. There was another door in the corridor. Theresa opened it and said, "Here's your water closet."

"What about a bathtub?"

"Madam told me I was to bring you up to the lounge when you'd seen the flat."

The cat was back on the landing but at the sight of us it shot off, disappearing on the second floor, where Theresa and I entered an L-shaped room. The woman sitting by the window was pretty in a style less appropriate to Fitzwilliam Square than to Madison Avenue: reddish blond hair not too carefully pinned up, green eyes that had a knowing expression when she smiled, or started to—she cut off her smile as if she'd suddenly thought better of it. Under her mohair coat she had on a pale blue wool dress. She also wore several rings, a heavy gold bracelet, and a gold watch. "Let's sit by the fireplace," she said, but no fire was lit, and she herself didn't sit. It was cold in the room, and I gladly accepted the offer of some sherry. She went over to a table of decanters and made a little ceremony of pouring; then standing by the fireplace, head tilted, fingers laced, she said, "It's an awkward business having people in one's house. It came on me before I knew what was happening. You see," she explained, "my dearest died seven years ago." I made some sound of sympathy which Mrs. Philbin didn't acknowledge. She had a story to tell; I sat back and let her get on with it. "He was a dentist, and the logical thing was to set his surgery to a colleague. Then I have a very dear friend, Lady Colby, whose son Mark has rooms with a classmate on the top floor. It was far too much space there for a single flat, and I've done up another which Mr. Shields has. He's doing an advanced degree at the College of Surgeons." That was the complete roster—or almost complete. Mrs. Philbin said, "The return room's a sweet place, don't you think?"

I said, "Yes, but there's no bath."

"You could use the one on the top floor. Or we might work something out about mine." I brought up the lack of a stove and she said, "You wouldn't want anything too elaborate?"

"Not too." I'd never done much cooking and I didn't feel entitled to press this point. "But I need something."

She laughed. "I know university students when it comes to meals." At this point the cat strolled into the room and over to the fire. Mrs. Philbin picked it up and introduced it. "This is Queen Maeve." Then she sat down in the chair opposite mine and, digging herself in, hugging the cat, she finished her story. "My own little girl would have entered university in two more years. My dearest Laura—she died of leukemia when she was eleven. My other poor dearest never got over it."

It was certainly all very tragic but it was all just as certainly a sales pitch. The message had come through to me— the box room was mine if I wanted it, and I did. For one thing it improved on without compromising my original vision—Fitzwilliam Square was an elegant district but it had certainly seen better days; and though the students and the doctor on the top floor sounded respectable rather than raffish, the dentist and the girl in the lab coat testified to the expedient nature of Stella Philbin's domestic arrangements; and I couldn't have asked for a more amusing landlady. Apart from all this, the flat satisfied something I'd discovered in myself only when I saw it, and that was a desire for continuity. I wanted to be part of a household—a past, present, and future, however lost the one and dubious the other two. I suppose I was homesick.

Mrs. Philbin said, "It would be a nice change having a young woman in the house."

"How much is the rent?" I asked, and she looked into the cold fireplace.

"Four pounds a week. Plus another pound to go towards the rates. Of course, all your linens would be supplied."

I pictured the disgust this bargain would have brought to Tomás O'Domhnaill's face, but the price seemed right to me, and so I took Stella Philbin's box room. As I stepped back out into Fitzwilliam Square, it struck me that renting a flat you'd heard about in a shop after spending only three and a half days in the city probably showed a lack of common sense, but not till later that day, when I first telephoned Oona Ross did I realize just how rash I'd been. Though Oona was discreet; for that matter so was I, not letting on that I'd actually rented a flat, only that I'd looked at one.

"How did you happen to hear of it?" Oona asked.

"From a woman in a shop." It sounded decidedly suspect, and I threw in, "A place called Plura Belle," for whatever the chic might be worth; and then shamelessly, certain of its snob value: "The flat's at number twenty Fitzwilliam Square."

"Stella Philbin's," Oona said in a changed voice. "I think you ought to hold off till you've talked to us. Are you free tonight?" I said I was. "Come and have supper," she said. "We're in a mews in the lane behind Merrion Square South. It's a sort of carriage house we've done up. You'll never find it but don't worry, we'll send someone to fetch you."

In the spring of that year I'd bought a brass-buttoned, navy blue flannel coat which stood out in the streets of Dublin like some form of American national costume. I'd put it aside permanently in favor of my raincoat but even so, that evening when I got off the elevator in the Shelbourne lobby, a young man came straight up to me and said, "Oona sent me after you. I'm Tom Wynne." I'd been expecting one of her daughters and I told him this. "Ah," he said, "they're all about their business, whatever that might be." He had a carefully modulated voice, and I wasn't surprised when he told me he was a singer. That accounted for the impassioned but monotonous quality of his conversation—like recitative, all of it about Oona: she was so brilliant and so busy, so generous and so disorganized. I wished I'd been left to find my own way and how easily I could have. It was only a couple of blocks to Merrion Square, and another short block brought us to the lane, a dirt road between two stone walls with a row of wicket doors. Parked next to one was a dusty Morris Minor that I recognized as the car Oona Ross and her daughters had been leaning against in the newspaper picture I'd seen. Then the wicket door flew open, and a child with straight black hair and hornrimmed glasses stuck her head out, yelled something, and disappeared again. "That's Madeleine," said Tom Wynne. "You must watch out for her, though it'll do you no good." I followed him into a small courtyard. Except for a storm door and a picture window, the carriage house didn't look done up to me. Inside it had aspects of both cave and castle—the walls were whitewashed brick, but the furniture was antique, the chairs upholstered surprisingly, or not surprisingly, in Irish tweed. Tom Wynne went into the recesses of this charming room and called, "Oona, I've brought you Ann Clarke!"

The woman who came running down the spiral staircase wasn't at all what I'd expected from the newspaper picture—that Oona had looked serene, but what struck me about the real Oona was her energy. She wore her hair knotted at the back, but the pins were sliding loose, and she was trying to do it up with one hand as she came over and gave me the other. "Beatrice didn't tell me you'd be so young!"

I said, "I'm twenty-six," though at the moment I felt much younger—not that Oona showed her forty-eight years. But she had an air of having used time better than most people.

"Twenty-six is when you begin not to know how young you are," she said. "Did you get the cheese, Tom?"

He said, "Not a shop from here to Ballsbridge had anything but the processed." If he seemed to speak in prepared speeches, when Oona spoke the effect was of someone choosing at random among any number of interesting and suitable ideas.

"Dublin is probably the only capital city in Europe where you can't be certain to find a shop that sells the country's own cheese," she said.

"Anyplace in England you'd have only to step round the corner," said Tom.

"And France—why," Oona said, "France would be worth the trip from here." She raised her voice. "How is our supper, Daise?"

"How do you expect roast chicken to be when it's sat around for half an hour?" There was real anger in this reply, and Oona looked intimidated.

"Daisy's raging at all of us," she said, "but she won't tell us why."

As we went and sat by the fire, a girl of fourteen or fifteen came down the staircase—this was Annabel, the middle daughter and the epitome of the Dublin girls' style, though except for her black hair there was no resemblance whatever to the child who'd looked out into the lane, nor to tall redhaired Daisy who at that point came in without a word and sat down on the floor.

"What did you think of Stella Philbin?" Oona asked me.

I said, "She struck me as cagey."

" 'Cagey!' " Annabel cried in broad Americanese, and everyone laughed.

"Which room did she show you?" asked Oona. I started to say box room and then decided that return room sounded better. "It's probably preferable to where she put us," Oona said.

"You lived in that house?" The effect coincidence has on people is out of proportion to what it offers—not the promise but only a suggestion that the correspondence of a couple of lives is the sign of a pattern to lives and events in general. And though it was obvious Oona didn't approve of Stella Philbin, I took the fact that they knew each other as another good sign. I said, "Isn't that amazing."

"After James died, I couldn't bear the farm. We came to Dublin and stayed for a while at Power's Hotel, but that was awful, too."

"Hotels are," I agreed.

But Oona said, "Not all of them. Sometimes the girls and I move into Buswell's just to pull ourselves together. It's heaven to me to get my breakfast and have the morning free to work."

Tom said, "Like it or not, Oona, you do your best work after seven o'clock at night."

I thought this sounded bossy, but Oona replied, "That's true." She liked advice for its own sake, for the way it involved her with someone else, though in the end she always did what she wanted. "I was thinking we'd go to Buswell's this weekend," she said. "You might come with us, Ann. Buswell's is no way near the price of the Shelbourne and it's very convenient. You could stay a week or two and get your bearings."

"I'd rather find a flat," I said, feeling guilty at the deception but secure in the knowledge of my box room.

"Don't rush into anything," said Oona. "That's where the girls and I went wrong. We were so unhappy at Power's, that when someone told us Stella Philbin was setting her top floor, we jumped at it. Her husband had just died, too. I must have thought that gave us something in common."

It was a ludicrous comparison. Oona was so vivid and direct, and Mrs. Philbin so veiled in affectation. I said, "What was wrong with the flat?"

"The floor was falling in!" spoke up Daisy.

Oona said, "Annabel was only eight, and Madeleine was just walking. I was afraid of my life they'd go crashing down into Stella Philbin's sitting room."

Annabel said, "She called it the lounge!"

"What's this she called flowers?" Oona said.

"Her blooms!" shouted the girls.

I hadn't particularly liked Mrs. Philbin but I felt obliged to defend her, for her defense and my own seemed to have something in common—mightn't "cagey" in its own way be just as bad as "blooms" and "lounge?" I said, "That was sad about the daughter."

"Oh God, the daughter!" said Daisy. "That was all we ever heard." She got to her feet. "Come and have the chicken."

It was a properly French chicken, fragrant with garlic and herbs. Oona said, "There's no one's cooking I enjoy as well as my own."

"All you do is start things," Daisy said.

Oona turned to me in all seriousness and said, "I'd like your opinion on something I came across in an advertisement—a sort of electric clock-cum-flask that you fill and plug in at night. Then in the morning it wakes you and boils the water, and there you have your tea."

"What a good idea," I said, though a combination clock and flask sounded to me like the sort of thing that would soon end up at the back of the closet. It seemed to strike Daisy the same way.

"Ah, for God's sake, mother," she said, "you're talking like grandmother."

Oona said to me, "You'll hear all about my mother."

I wondered if this meant an exchange, my story for hers, and I didn't relish the idea. My mother with her ecclesiastical friends, my father and his gambling—what it really amounts to on both their parts is antisocial behavior. I'm sensitive about this and I was thinking of how best to gloss over it, when the youngest girl suddenly reappeared, snatched a piece of meat from Oona's plate, and then ran off again.

Oona called, "Come and eat something, Madeleine!"

Annabel said, "Catch her when she comes down for the sweet."

Oona put her hand to her mouth. "I forgot the cake!" She sounded concerned in the same way and to the same degree that she'd been about the troubles with Stella Philbin and with her mother, and even about the clock-flask. My own concerns in life were ranked—love, family, social life, work, money—and I began to wonder whether torrents of undifferentiated feeling were really for me. I had other reservations based on the fancy furniture, the garlicky chicken, even or maybe especially the girls' names. There were plenty of Daisys and Annabels and Madeleines back in New York. I wanted to meet someone like Tomás O'Domhnaill and I didn't think I was likely to do so in the cosmopolitan atmosphere of Oona Ross's mews. As I left that evening, Oona said to me, "We must see each other often," and I agreed, adding to myself, "Not likely." It was a heady sensation to feel, in the face of such a pleasant prospect, that I could take it or leave it.

The next day I presented myself at Trinity College, my home base and a disappointment. The buildings around the courtyard looked rundown. It also dawned on me that I'd crossed the ocean with no other definite purpose than to go to school. Still, I wanted to make a good impression but I was out of practice, and the assistant registrar was unsympathetic. "Well, Miss Clarke," she said, "what do you propose to do here at Trinity?"

I said, "I thought I might try Irish."

"The Irish language?" She looked skeptical.

"And maybe a course in Irish literature," I hastened to add.

She noted this on my application and took off her glasses. "About accommodations."

I said, "I've already rented a flat."

She put the glasses back on. "Women students must live in residences approved by the College," she said as if she were reading from a handbook.

"But I'm not a full-time student," I pointed out. "Besides, nobody mentioned that when I first wrote. Otherwise I might not have applied." It was a shot in the dark, and so I was surprised when it hit home; but of course a student withdrawn meant fees lost, explanations to be made, blame to be shouldered.

"Where is this flat?" she asked. I told her, and she wrote down the address. "Term begins the week after next. Once you start classes you'll be assigned a tutor." She began studying the next application.

I was a bit insulted as I got up and found my way out of the building. I'd been made to feel like a suspicious character when in fact I was perfectly sincere about wanting to study Irish at Trinity—sincere but unrealistic. I saw myself becoming fluent in the language I'd caught scraps of when I was in Cork, I imagined conversations in which I made distinctions or even jokes with Tomás O'Domhnaill and his friends, and I pictured myself bringing back with me to New York the Irish language, a matchless souvenir.

Four The day I left the Shelbourne, the girl with the auburn hair was off duty, but they were all alike, those Shelbourne girls. Informed of my forwarding address, this one said, "You'll be close enough to drop in and check the post yourself."

"I'd rather have it forwarded," I said, as if the Shelbourne would figure not at all in the life on which I was embarked.

It was eleven o'clock, the middle of a business morning, when the taxi dropped me off at number twenty. I rang one of the anonymous bells, and Theresa instantly appeared; she'd been scrubbing the hall floor. Sticking her cigarette in the corner of her mouth she picked up one of my suitcases, and I picked up the other and followed her across the dry patches and upstairs. The girl in the lab coat was at her desk, and Theresa formally introduced us: "Miss Ann Clarke, Miss Dinah Kenyon."

I said, "Kenyon doesn't sound like an Irish name."

"It's not. I'm the dread *Sassenach—Sassenach* is Irish for English." The doorbell rang. Theresa dropped my bag and went back downstairs. "Let me give you a hand," Dinah said and she came out from behind her desk and picked up my suitcase, and we went into the box room. The first thing I noticed was that the gray velvet bedspread had been exchanged for an older, shabbier model in a color that could once have been either rust or rose. What struck me next was a more serious breach of faith. "For heaven's sake, there's no stove!"

"And you were promised one?" said Dinah. It wasn't so much a question as the recognition of some not really surprising fact above and beyond that of the missing stove.

"I suppose it's coming," I said.

Dinah's phone rang, and she said, "I'd better get that."

"If you see Theresa," I said, "would you tell her I'd like to talk to her?"

"You bet."

I was relieved when she left and I could take stock of the place without having to pretend it was better than it looked, for the cold light of morning had made my second impression rather different from the first. I saw that the wallpaper was peeling in a couple of places; in a corner of the ceiling there was a large leak stain; and my linens, which lay across the substitute bedspread, consisted of two worn sheets, two matted blankets, and two frayed towels striped in garish multicolor. Rather than dwell on all this I began putting away my clothes and was well into the second case when Mrs. Philbin arrived with my stove. "A little paraffin stove," she called it.

There were, I knew, such things as electric hot plates, inexpensive and satisfactory, and I was angry at having this gadget foisted on me instead. "What's paraffin?" I asked her.

"I believe you people call it kerosene." She began fiddling with the stove and got the plate unscrewed. "There—when you've put in the paraffin oil you replace this and set your saucepan on top." I asked how safe it was, and she pouted in a practiced way. "Perfectly, I should think."

"I mean having paraffin oil in the room."

"Do you smoke?" she asked, and I had to admit I didn't. "Then there's nothing to worry about."

"It has no oven."

Mrs. Philbin straightened her handsome shoulders. "You really intend to cook for yourself, do you?"

I said, "I want to at least be able to."

"Then we must fix you up with something proper. In the meantime I suppose this will do?" I said I supposed so, and she told me, "Should you need anything else, just ask Ta. She looks after all the guests."

Ta—it was a fancy nickname for a plain person like Theresa, but calling boarders "guests" was something more than fanciful. Confusing that issue could have complications that I meant to forestall as I reached for my handbag and said, "Shall I give you the rent now?"

"Ta will take it," said Mrs. Philbin.

That afternoon I went and bought myself two crisp new sheets and three yellow towels at Brown Thomas on Grafton Street, but I outfitted my kitchen at Clery's on the north side, the cheap side of the Liffey; there I got an aluminum saucepan, a skillet and a kettle, some plain white dishes, some stainless steel cutlery. I also bought a handwoven rug, and a pottery mug and bowl like the ones I'd seen at the Driscolls' apartment in New York.

In the evening Theresa took me up to the top floor and demonstrated the use of the water heater on the bathtub: you lit a match, turned a knob, and put the flame to the jet. A week went by before I attempted this simple operation for myself; then one night I rolled a towel around my soap and facecloth and made my way to the top of the house. I was alone there but not knowing that I hastily performed the simple operation in the wrong sequence. There was a bang and a flash of green light, and a pane of glass shattered in the window beside the tub. I threw my clothes back on and ran down to Theresa in the basement, and together we went up to Mrs. Philbin who at that moment was soaking in her own tub which stood in a sort of frosted glass shed built into a corner of her bedroom. Theresa called out, "Madam, Miss Clarke has blown the geyser on the top-floor bath!"

There was one of the silences that Mrs. Philbin would let accumulate between herself and unpleasantness. "Then," she said, "Miss Clarke will need another lesson on the bathtub."

I finally got a stove that could be called proper, though at first that cast-iron box with legs like stilts looked dangerous to me. But on it I learned to make *coq au vin*, I grilled pounds of lamb chops and fried countless sausages and eggs, I put on innumerable kettles for endless cups of tea.

The oven I used only once, the time I made dinner for Tony Shields who lived on the top floor. Tony was doing his advanced degree in orthopedics, having left a practice as well as a wife and two children back in County Cavan. "I've a five-year plan like the Russians," he told me when we met. "In five years' time I'll be a consultant with a post at Vincent's Hospital and a house in Donnybrook." In the meantime he was out all day at the College of Surgeons; at night he stayed at the National Library till it closed, and when he returned to his room at the top of Mrs. Philbin's he sometimes dropped in first on me. He was the one other "guest" I got to know. Lady Colby's son and his roommate only passed me in the hall, and only occasionally; they were both very short and usually dressed in jodhpurs and according to Tony the two of them were training to be jockeys. Tony also confirmed what I'd learned from Oona Ross about the top floor of the house. "One of these days I'm going right through the flipping boards into Mrs. P's lap," he told me. "Which would probably suit her fine."

"Is she that type?" I asked.

"You have to watch yourself with Mrs. Stella Philbin," was all I got from Tony. I think he compared my journey from New York with his own up from Cavan, and though we'd arrived with somewhat the same purpose, there the comparison ended. He was in deadly earnest about his studies, whereas after the first meeting, I never went back to my class in Irish literature, though it took me longer to drop out of the Irish language thanks to the professor, a tall gaunt man named Proinsias O'Laoghaire. I still take pleasure in my mastery of that name: Prin-shus O'Leary. He used to wear a tweed cap and a brown gabardine overcoat that looked as if he kept it rolled up in a corner. After taking these off he'd reach into the pocket of his waistcoat for a small box wrapped in rubberbands and from the box he's remove the strapless face of a lady's wristwatch, propping it against his briefcase. The close attention I gave this remarkable routine lingered on into the lecture and led Proinsias O'Laoghaire to take me for a promising student, which I might have been if three weeks into the term I hadn't come down with a cold. When I returned two weeks later I realized at once that I'd never be able to make up the work but I kept on going to class. Proinsias O'Laoghaire avoided my eyes which I regretted, but otherwise it was a relief to have loosened my connection with Trinity College. I'd thought the university would be necessary to me, that without it my days would make no sense, but instead Trinity came to be little more than an alibi. When anyone asked what I was doing in Dublin, I'd say, "I'm a student."

I'd been installed in the box room about a week when Dinah said, "Look, Ann, I've spoken to Mr. Hughes, and he says it's perfectly all right with him if you get your calls on our telephone." She was a nice girl—kind and practical, open and tactful; we used to have polite, easy conversations. "Daddy worked for Guinness's in London," she told me. "He was transferred here when I was six; then when I was seventeen, they sent him back to England."

"You didn't want to go along?" I asked.

"I had another year at the College of Music," she said. "Besides, all my friends were Irish. And I suppose I'd got used to it here."

I said, "I'm getting used to it myself." To be completely beautiful things must have an element of the habitual, and it wasn't till I was settled in there that I truly began to appreciate Dublin. You had only to follow the crowd: through Stephen's Green with its symmetrical flower beds, and the bandstand where deckchairs were stacked, and the pond with the ducks; or down Grafton Street—that perversely narrow and crooked main thoroughfare lined with misleadingly unpretentious shops; or over to O'Connell Street, lingering on O'Connell Bridge to watch the dirty swans on the Liffey and savor the view to the west where Dublin could be seen petering out like a village.

"The trouble with Ireland," said Dinah, "is it grows on

you." She had a way of using out-of-date American slang that made her seem old fashioned or even old though she was my age to the month. "Would you like a bite of dinner tonight?" she asked me one morning. "A friend of mine's coming. Or is this too short notice? You'll be making do with cottage pie."

Dinah lived in a basement flat on Pembroke Street, one of two avenues from Fitzwilliam Square onto Leeson Street. "Mind the step," she said that evening as I followed her into a big room full of cumbersome furniture. It was like walking into the showroom of a third-rate auctioneer, and Dinah knew it. "Most of this stuff is mummy's and daddy's leavings. Let me have your coat," she said and she brought me into a bedroom full of more huge furniture; as we started back to the sitting room, the doorbell rang. "That'll be Molly," said Dinah.

Her friend Molly Corcoran was five feet ten, and the kind of tall girl who'd learned to tuck herself up though she hadn't quite got her breezy personality under control. "All right, Dinah, go on with the supper," she said, sitting down on a stool by the fireplace. "Ann's going to tell me all about herself. Now, Ann, what are you doing here in Ireland?"

"Studying at Trinity," I said.

"Don't tell me!" said Molly. "I was sure it was a tragic love affair, and you'd come to us to heal your broken heart."

Dinah called from the kitchen, "Molly, you've been reading *Women's Own* again."

"That rag," said Molly. "Of course, Ann, your American magazines are tops. I work for an ad agency and I'll grant you that doesn't mean I know a damn thing about the publishing game, but I think I do, and if you ask me your mags are it." I began to see where Dinah got her American slang. "Fancy, there you were at the heart of it and left it all behind," said Molly. "Do you miss New York?"

I said, "Not really."

"What do you do with yourself here?"

Sedentary pleasures appeal to me best. Wherever I am, I

love to watch things and think about them but after a month in Dublin I'd reached a saturation point, and the sights and sounds accumulating in my mind had begun seeping over into the notebook I'd bought for my lectures at Trinity. Every morning I sat down at the white wicker table and filled several pages with conversations I'd overheard, descriptions of people I saw in the street or in one or another of the Dublin *cafés*, plus observations that I thought of as the essence of my new experience. I attacked these subjects with a passion that now strikes me as the purest effort of any sort I've ever made, for my only purpose was to try and hold onto the sights that caught my attention and the emotions that flared up in me as I moved through the city. The old woman waiting at the bus stop, wearing a tan coat with a flight of silver geese on each lapel; the man in Bewley's, ordering a cp of Bovril and advising the rest of us at the table, "It's the one thing beats the influenza"; the child in the fish store, crying her heart out because she'd lost the ten shillings that was supposed to pay for her pound of plaice—all my energy and the better part of my day went into these assignments I gave myself, but it wasn't anything I felt like talking about. "I guess I waste a lot of time," I told Molly.

"Supper's ready!" Dinah brought in a steaming dish, and we followed her over to the table. "Now, Ann, this is cottage pie," Dinah said.

It turned out to be ground beef and vegetables under a mashed potato crust. "You'll have to tell me how to make it," I said.

"What tact," said Molly. "You must be a big hit with our Stella."

"Molly!"

"Now Dinah," said Molly, "I'm sure Ann has learned for herself what a bitch that woman is."

I said, "Actually I've been trying to make up my mind about her."

Dinah said, "She's a strange woman really. Of course she's had heaps of trouble."

Molly said, "Dinah's such a mug. You're such a mug, Dinah."

Dinah's charming discretion was at odds with her absolute honesty. I tried to let her off the hook. "Don't worry, I'll learn for myself."

Dinah said, "Watch yourself with her, Ann. She runs hot and cold—one day she'll be sweet as sugar and the next thing you know she's perfectly poisonous."

Molly swallowed hastily and went into gales of laughter.

Dinah said, "What *is* the matter with you?"

"It just occurred to me—what with living at Stella Philbin's and in Fitzwilliam, you might say Ann's landed in the thick of it." I was expecting to be told of a rash of burglaries, when Molly said, "You've heard of Bond Street in London?"

I said, "Where the expensive shops are?"

"Also the expensive whores. Well," said Molly, "Fitzwilliam Square is Dublin's Bond Street."

Dinah said, "Many a night I've been followed by a cruising automobile."

"One time," said Molly, "a fellow came clear round the Square after me, opening his door every few feet, but it turned out to be Rory in his brother's car."

"Rory is Molly's true love," Dinah said, but Molly denied this though not very convincingly.

"I've known Rory MacDonagh for ages," she said. "We're pals."

A good address with a racy reputation struck me as ideal. "But is it safe at night by yourself?" I asked.

"Safe as church," Molly said. "They give up when they see you're not in business. There're loads that are."

"Mind you," said Dinah, "you must look sharp, show them you know what you're about."

Molly reached for her handbag, took out a pack of cigarettes, and offered them around. "Sometimes it's good fun," she said. "The girls get into terrific fights and start pulling hair."

Dinah said, "That's enough, Molly. Ann will get the

wrong idea. More pie anyone?"

I said, "I couldn't."

Molly said, "Full up, Di."

"I didn't make a sweet," Dinah said. "I thought we'd have Irish coffees."

"Ah," said Molly, "thank God for the Americans who invented it and the English who picked it up. What would us poor Paddies do without you?"

We were, I think, good examples of the three different cultures that produced us: Molly shrewd and funny, Dinah sensible and sympathetic, and conscientious me—I was embarrassed at having had nothing legitimate to say that I was doing with all my spare time, but neither of them seemed to think the less of me. "Now you know one more person," Dinah said to me as Molly and I left that night.

Five Dinah, Molly, Proinsias O'Laoghaire, the people in my Irish class (all four English and years younger than I), Tony Shields, Mrs. Philbin—it wasn't exactly what you'd call a set. A couple of times I thought of getting in touch with Oona Ross but I felt sheepish about having to admit that against her better judgment I'd rented Stella Philbin's return room and besides, I knew that sooner or later some new element would emerge to make things coalesce and become dynamic. In the meantime I was reluctant to give up the beautiful sense of strangeness that had been conferred on my life by virtue of its uneventfulness. Not even letters from home could spoil that. "Things are as good as can be expected . . ." Barbara would write. And my mother: "I can hardly believe it's only _six_ weeks since you left! Are you _warm_

enough? Do you *like* Trinity College? . . ."

I wrote in my notebook: *On the edge of all happiness lies the consciousness of the sorrows of others, ready to contaminate.* But I had an antidote to the contamination—the streets of Dublin. Those regular ranks of gray houses seemed to suggest that trouble was the natural state of human affairs and that you could best deal with trouble by bearing it in mind. Though there was plenty of life in those streets. People were always running into their friends, especially on Grafton Street, where I found myself constantly stepping off the sidewalk to avoid groups who'd stopped to gossip or to transact a quick bit of business. I was very much aware of being a stranger in the midst of all this fellowship but I was confident my time would come, and it did one afternoon at the beginning of October. I'd left the National Library and was waiting for a chance to cross Kildare Street, when something made me look twice at the man in front of me. It turned out to be Tomás O'Domhnaill. I spoke to him, and he looked around and stared at me for a second; then with a nod at the library, he said, "So here's where you've been hiding." I denied that I'd been hiding anywhere, and he said, "Well, you're hard enough to locate."

"Where were you looking?" I asked.

He said, "I wasn't actually. I just happened to inquire in one or two pubs."

A thrill of interest went through me, and I thought: He *was* looking for me. "You should have tried Bewley's," I said.

"I haven't been there in ten years."

"You don't know what you're missing."

He drew me away from the curb and asked what I'd been up to, and I told him about the flat in Fitzwilliam. "That's very grand," he said.

"Not very." I thought of Dinah outside the box-room door and of the dentist downstairs. "But it's what I wanted."

"There's a lot to be said for that, isn't there—getting what you want."

This sort of philosophizing made him seem to have a

thoughtful turn of mind, but in fact when Tomás became philosophical it usually meant he was stalling for time, which was apparent to me as we stood there. But I played along. "I don't think there's much to be said for getting anything besides what you want."

"That's a very modern point of view."

"I'm from a very modern country."

"Where were you this afternoon?"

"At my Irish class."

"*An ólfaidh tú deoch liom?*"

I said, "We haven't come to that yet."

" 'Will you have a drink with me?' " he translated. I said I would, and he asked me the time; when I told him it was half past four, there was a subtle change in his manner. "Come along," he said, and we crossed the street to a phone box. I had to wait while he made a string of calls, but it was pleasant standing there, watching people pass by, feeling myself about to move among them and discover the city's true life. I was in high spirits by the time Tomás took my arm and said, "We're off."

He brought me to a pub called Hanlon's, an austere sort of place that was newly but shoddily done up. Before we'd ordered drinks we were joined by his friend Liam MacMahon who greeted Tomás in Irish and then kissed my hand.

"What will you have?" Tomás asked me.

I felt that this was the real start of my Dublin life and, wanting it to be a good start—also having a kind of technical interest in how that life would differ from the life I knew—I asked, "What are you having?"

Tomás said, "A pint."

I asked what a pint was, and Liam said, "Naiveté to a point, my dear."

"A pint is always a pint of stout," said Tomás. "You don't want that, sure you don't."

I said, "No, I couldn't drink a whole pint but I'd like a glass."

Tomás looked as if the idea were ridiculous but he gave

the order; then he said to Liam, "Ann has got herself a flat in Fitzwilliam. She's doing Irish at Trinity."

Liam addressed a few words of Irish to me; I lifted my shoulders, and he and Tomás went on speaking their harsh language till I said, "That's not fair."

"Forgive us, my dear," said Liam. "We were only saying we might go on to Neary's."

"Drink up," said Tomás.

But I left most of my glass of stout and at Neary's I ordered a beer. "You mean a lager. You just had beer," Tomás informed me.

Neary's was crowded, and the crowd seemed to be drawn from a single broad grouping of age and class— youthful to middle-aged, up-and-coming to prosperous. Half the people there knew Liam and Tomás, and another table was added on to ours, and more chairs were fetched. Of those who joined us, three stand out in my mind—Sean Kelly, a painter; Myles O'Grady who was missing a front tooth and apparently unmindful of this; Martin Brodie who was a poet. What luck, I thought as I sat there among them. The day before I'd been the solitary stranger; now I was with people who, if I'd passed them on Grafton Street, would have struck me as the very sort I'd have wanted to get to know, people who were obviously the real thing, which meant for a start that the conversation kept veering off into Irish. "Are all of you native speakers?" I asked Tomás.

"Not at all. As a matter of fact Martin's a Jew." He turned to his friends and said, "What do you think of Ann?"

Martin said, "She has a Galway face."

"I'd have thought Cork," said Liam. "Brown eyes are commoner there."

I learned that evening what a wealth of this kind of information Tomás and his friends possessed. They could quote from memory the works of obscure Irish poets; they were walking catalogs of Irish traditional music and musicians; they were genealogical experts. "You certainly love your country," I said at one point.

"To be civilized," said Tomás, "a man must be thoroughly familiar with his own district."

By this definition and probably most others, Tomás and his friends could certainly be called civilized but they also had a cruel streak which showed up later, when Liam looked at his watch and said, "It's half nine. I must ring my wife." And he got up and left the table.

I turned to Tomás and said, "He's married?"

Ten minutes went by before Liam returned. "I couldn't get through," he said. "Joan must have left the phone off the hook. She often does when she's tired and doesn't want to be bothered."

His look of mixed relief and guilt told a different story, the real one: He'd missed dinner without letting his wife know, and she was furious. This changed the character of the evening, and I said to Tomás, "Hadn't we better leave?"

"You've not finished your lager," he pointed out.

"I've had enough." I swayed as I got up to go to the ladies' room and then I tripped on the stairs but when I looked in the mirror, my face struck me as sober enough. I splashed my cheeks with cold water, found a clean patch of the roller towel to dry them on, and went back to the table. There were two newcomers, a couple of girls; one of them, an Indian wearing a pink sari under her raincoat, was deep in conversation with Liam; the other girl, who was Irish, had a way of hesitating over some of her words and emphasizing others that struck me as an effort to get attention. I asked Tomás who she was, and he told me her name was Aideen Fitzgerald, and I said, "I don't like her." I was really feeling the beer.

Shortly after this the girls left, and Liam leaned across the table to me and said, "I understand you didn't like Aideen." I turned to Tomás, who looked at me rather coldly. "It's too bad you feel that way," said Liam, "because she was telling me she wished she could help you feel at home."

I understood that some question of loyalty was at stake, that Aideen being Irish had the prior claim. In a vague effort to advance my own cause, or at least to keep Tomás's attention, I told him I was hungry, and he said, "We'll soon be leaving." But he and Liam and I stayed till Neary's closed; then when we were out on the street, Tomás said, "Will we get something to eat, Liam?"

They settled on a restaurant called The Acropolis, just the other side of the Green and within easy walking distance, but Tomás insisted on driving. Then he couldn't remember where he'd left the Volkswagen, and we traipsed around for ten minutes before he located it around the corner from Jury's Hotel. When we got to The Acropolis, the lights were out, and the shades were drawn, but Liam knocked, and a man came to the door. Liam said, "Can you let us have something to eat, Teddy?"

"We're closed," the man said but with the air of someone who often found himself in the position of giving in and had learned to do it quickly. "I suppose I can give you a *pasta*, Liam." He led us to the back of the restaurant and lit the candle on a corner table before going out to the kitchen.

I said, "It's like a speakeasy."

"Ah," said Liam, "your nation's darkest hour."

Teddy returned to the table with a bottle of wine and said, "This is Greek wine, Liam. I want you to try it."

"Teddy's Greek," Tomás told me.

"Is he Irish, too?" I asked.

Tomás said, "Don't talk rubbish."

I was indignant. "Martin Brodie's Irish and Jewish. Why can't someone be Irish and Greek?"

Teddy filled our wine glasses and said, *"Slainte,"* his Greek accent making it "Slantey." We all drank, and he asked, "What do you think of the wine?"

Liam said, "It's not bad. Mind you, it's not good, but it's not bad." To make up for this, I told Teddy I loved his wine, and he topped up my glass. We finished that bottle and another half; we ate two plates of *pastitsio* and drank a pot of coffee, and I had a dish of chocolate ice cream. In the middle of the meal Tomás suddenly got up and left the table. When he came back, Liam said, "Are you feeling all right, Tommy?"

"I feel bloody awful," said Tomás.

I said, "I wonder why I don't. After all that beer and wine I should be sick as a dog." But I was fine, though when we left The Acropolis the fresh air felt good, and I suggested we walk to Fitzwilliam. "I'd like the exercise," I said. I was really a little worried about Tomás's driving, but again he insisted on taking the car, and we drove at top speed through the quiet streets to Fitzwilliam.

As we parked in front of number twenty, Liam said, "Ann, I neglected to use the conveniences at Teddy's place. Could I trouble you?"

"All right," I said, "but we mustn't make a sound. This is a quiet house." It was also pitch dark. The streetlamp shining obliquely through the fanlight made a pattern of pale openwork that was all we had to guide us up the stairs to the box room. There Tomás began walking around touching things—my earthenware, my white dishes, the striped rug at the foot of the daybed. "How much do you pay for this place?" he asked.

"Three pounds a week," I said, but the lie wasn't ambitious enough.

"You've been had," said Tomás and he sat down on the daybed. I brought Liam out to the water closet; when I returned, Tomás patted the bed and said, "Come join me."

I was of two minds about him. I thought him attractive but I also found something lacking in him, something simple like courtesy having to do with something more important like character. But that night the lack didn't strike me as beyond repair, and I sat down beside him, and we put our arms around each other and began to kiss. After a minute or two we heard the door in the corridor open. I started to break away, but he held onto me, saying, "Don't move."

I was lying back on the bed with Tomás bending over

me when Liam returned. He said, "I beg your pardon." But Tomás wanted us to be found that way; as soon as we were, he sat up.

Mrs. Philbin might think of her tenants as guests and her house as private, but to me the place was a glorified office. Most days I woke to the ringing of Dinah's telephone and though I'd learned to sleep past it, the morning after I was out with Tomás the phone woke me on the first ring and made my head ache. I got up and put on some clothes and went out to Dinah. "I don't suppose you have any aspirin," I said. "I've the worst hangover."

She opened a desk drawer and handed me the bottle. "I hope it was worth it."

"I'm not so sure." I went back to my room and took two aspirin and made some coffee and brought Dinah a cup.

"Who is he, and do you like him?" she asked.

"Someone I met in Cork who turned up here," I said. "And I can't tell—all we did was drink."

"Irishmen, Ann, come in two varieties," she said, "those who live at home with mum and those who live at the pub. Quite honestly, I think you've struck the better sort."

I said, "I hope I didn't wake the whole house coming in."

"I doubt it," said Dinah. "Mrs. Philbin's bedroom is on the third floor. Of course Theresa sleeps in the basement— not that Theresa would care, but if you made too much noise, she'd have wanted to warn you."

In spite of the hangover I went to my Irish class and afterwards I put in some time at the National Library. When I got home, Theresa met me at the door with a gleam in her good eye. "A gentleman's here to see you," she said. "I've put him in reception." This had been the dining room of the house and it was still furnished with side chairs and a Queen Anne table stacked at intervals with back issues of magazines. Tomás was standing there going through an old *Punch*. He wore a tweed overcoat that was cut as full as a cape and made him look incongruously swaggering, and I was thrown off by this and by the fact of his turning up. I'd rather have had some time, so that the desire to see him might build up again, but Tomás didn't go in for strategy.

I said, "I didn't know you were staying over in Dublin."

"Nor did I." He put down the *Punch*. "Get your things. We're meeting Liam at The White Horse."

I said, "I haven't recovered from last night."

"Hair of the dog," said Tomás. "There's nothing to beat it." I had no real desire nor any good reason to turn him down, and I went upstairs to leave my books in the box room. Tomás came along, taking the stairs two at a time. "Three pounds for this!" he said as he followed me into the flat.

Close quarters foster intimacy, but when he reached out and grabbed me, I said, "Stop that."

"Why?" he asked innocently.

He was going too fast, but that was how the whole evening went—pell-mell from The White Horse which was down by the river, on to Conway's in Moore Street, and on again to Neary's. Here friends of Liam and Tomás materialized as they had the night before, and two more tables were pushed together. As I got up for this to be accomplished, Martin Brodie put his hands on my waist and lifted me off the floor. "Now you can tell people you've been picked up in a bar," he said.

"What do you think of Ann?" Tomás asked again.

Martin said, "The question is, what does Ann think of us?"

I said, "I haven't made up my mind." But I had several opinions on the subject. Tomás and his friends struck me as excitingly authentic and dangerously careless, though their general irresponsibility also amused me and acted as an emotional safety catch—I supposed them not to be trusted, didn't do so, and thus felt comfortable with them. Above all, I was impressed by their solidarity, though I also distrusted this and was slightly put off by it. "Do you always go around together?" I asked Tomás.

He relayed this question to Liam who said, "My dear Ann, it's the nature of friendship to cling, is it not?"

I was no more able to finish all the lagers that were ordered for me than I'd been on the previous night and so I began to be left out of every second round, but in other respects that evening was a copy of the first up till closing time; then as the barman began to call, "Time!" there was a consultation at the table, after which Tomás went and bought a dozen stout.

"What's happening?" I asked.

"There's a party at Kevin Keating's," Liam said. "Kevin has a big flat on Leeson Street."

The big flat was three rooms, no way near enough space for the crowd who showed up and tried to circulate. It looked to me as if half the pubs in Dublin were emptied out there, and I asked Tomás how word got around. "Dublin is a small city," he said. Most of the girls and some of the fellows looked like students, but there were a few middle-aged men in the crowd, one of whom Tomás identified as an assistant to someone in the government. "A devotee of traditional music." This referred to an overheated fiddler industriously playing in a corner of the room. Tomás sighed and said, "I suppose I must search out a bottle of lager for you."

"I'll do it myself." I set off for the kitchen and met Martin Brodie going in the same direction. "Are you enjoying yourself, Ann?" he asked.

"Not particularly," I said.

"These occasions aren't really for enjoyment," he said, "they're for drinking. Do you not drink?"

"Not enough."

"Nor do I," he said. "Sometimes I have to pretend to be drunk for kindness' sake."

"Kindness," I said, "there's a neglected virtue."

"Are you kind?" he asked.

"When I can be."

"That's the trouble with the virtues," he said. "They're damned inconvenient." I liked Martin. He was more serious than Tomás and more sincere than Liam; he was also independent. "Well," he said, "I'll be off soon anyway."

"Maybe we can drive you." I was hoping to make my own getaway, but Martin was no help.

"Don't bother Tommy. The walk will clear my head."

On the way back to the living room I ran into Aideen Fitzgerald and from her hostile manner understood that someone had passed along the remark I'd made about her. I was sorry since I no longer had the conviction that what I'd said was true; Aideen now struck me as smart and interesting. I shook my head and complained about the noise, and she said, "You're hard to please, aren't you?"

I don't like milling around, having to pretend I'm enjoying myself if I'm not, and getting involved in conversations that go nowhere. When I'd had enough I made my way back to Tomás and said, "Let's leave," and to my surprise he agreed.

"We'll just find Liam. I promised him a lift."

Liam was in a corner arguing with Myles. "You and Ann go along," he said distractedly. "I'll get a ride somewhere."

After all those people, it was odd suddenly being alone with Tomás out in the silent, foreign city. When we got in the car, he went to put his arm around me, but I moved out of reach, telling him, "You're a bad enough driver."

"I'm an excellent driver," he said and in a burst of speed and bravado he went the length of Leeson Street and around to my door. "I'll see you inside," he said, and I supposed he had some idea of coming in again himself. The major effect on me of growing up surrounded by priests and nuns is that when some such circumstances arise, I feel compelled to do what strikes me as the worldly thing regardless of how I feel, and when Tomás asked himself in for a cup of tea, I agreed though with a stipulation.

"You have to be quiet." Against the darkness in the hall, a small, pale shape stood out straight ahead—this was Queen Maeve sitting halfway up the staircase, but Tomás didn't notice the cat till she bolted, startling him so that he missed his footing and cried out. I whispered, "Be still!"

"I damn near broke my neck!" he complained loudly, and I rushed him the rest of the way to the box room, where he made himself at home on the daybed, while I put the kettle on. "Come join me," he said as he had the night before. I went and sat beside him, and we began kissing. Then we lay back.

Ideally I'd choose to be virtuous, for reasons having to do with privacy and the length of time it takes to feel you know someone—unless, of course, I'm in love. I wasn't in love with Tomás but I felt that with a little encouragement I could be. On the other hand I didn't want to be railroaded, and when the water began to boil, I said, "I've got to get the kettle." He let go of me, and I went and shut off the gas and made the tea. I heard him moving around; when I turned, he'd drawn back the bedcovers and was getting undressed. I said, "What do you think you're doing?" With the man in New York I'd loved, the man who was married, there'd been long discussions about what appeared to Tomás to be understood.

"I'm getting into bed," he said and he came and put his arms around me. "Won't you come, too?"

"It's my bed," I reminded him.

"Well then, won't you invite me in?"

I remembered how he'd struck me when we met in Cork—straightforward, self-contained, skeptical. In Dublin I'd walked the streets thinking about him and measuring the men I saw against my image of him. I'd thought him perfectly typical of his kind, and he seemed that still, though now I understood that I had yet to piece together what his kind was. At the moment he looked slightly embarrassed, standing there in his undershirt, and there was something attractive about this. Modesty can be physically disarming in the way that discretion is intellectually so. "Leave your tea and come along, Ann," he said.

I said, "Oh, all right."

Six *Tomás has never taken an attitude towards himself. He sees the man he is not in terms of some image of his own character but always in relation to other men, with the result that his real self gets lost, and his particular qualities—genuine good nature, enthusiasm, underlying decency (the great rake act notwithstanding), loyalty—all this is reduced to a nondescript, hail-fellow-well-met, devil-may-care sort of attitude.*

That was what I wrote in my notebook on November 22, wondering as I made the note how Tomás had assessed me. An American girl—I strongly suspected he'd left it at that, though he'd had plenty of opportunity to study me. Every week or so there was a phone call from him, or when I returned from the library, Theresa would come to the box room to tell me that Mr. O'Domhnaill was down in reception. Theresa liked Tomás, and in some ways they reminded me of each other. They were both country people and both loved intrigue—her look of complicity as she gave me her message would resemble the secretive look that was characteristically his. You'd have thought from his expression that Tomás was planning some remarkable surprise, but the evenings we spent together were all alike and all basically like the first though between pubs we usually managed to have something to eat. But the cast of characters was invariable: Tomás and Liam and I, Martin Brodie, Myles O'Grady—that was the nucleus. Then there was Sean Kelly, always with paint-stained fingers and an abstracted look, as if those of us around him were so much line and color; and there was the crowd from *Radio Eireann* who seemed to be perpetually drunk; and Martin's literary friends who spoke with passion of the magazines they were trying to start or of other magazines that despite their best efforts were about to fold. Most of these people I never got to know but I can still see their faces, or rather one face—the Irish face with its depth of expression that spoke to me of native wit and intelligence, of an extraordinary grasp of life and a keener appreciation of it than I was used to, plus the contempt for any interpretation that was on the one hand less riotous and on the other hand less austere than that which informed its own features. Sometimes the Irish face seemed to me merely more responsive than the face I saw in the mirror, or faces in American magazines that I'd buy for the purpose of such comparisons, and I'd ask myself if Irish people were more accurately tuned to life than we were. Other times I wondered if the Irish expression were an indication of a more human, more fallible, simpler, and yet nobler attitude than my own. Still other times I decided all this was my imagination.

At some point in those evenings I spent with Tomás and his friends, Aideen Fitzgerald always turned up, usually in the rooms full of people that we made our way to when the pubs closed. The look she and I would exchange made me feel as if I'd met my nemesis, and I got the sense that she felt the same way and enjoyed it, though I didn't. What struck me about the parties themselves was the absence, as far as I could tell, of real bonds among the people there. I couldn't picture any of them meeting in each other's houses for dinner or drinks. I couldn't imagine them going to the theater together. Their link was the city itself and the need to find a place there where they could go after hours. Occasionally I rebelled against this regime. "Let's go to a movie," I once said to Tomás when we were sitting in Neary's.

He gave me a look of disbelief; then he leaned across the table and told Liam, "Ann wants to go to the pictures!"

Liam said, "What on earth for?"

I said, "For a change."

Liam said, "When you've got a good thing, stick with it, baby. Isn't that what you say in your country?"

Another time I asked Tomás to go with me to *Playboy of the Western World*, which was on at the Gaiety. He informed me that everyone had seen it dozens of times, but I said, "I haven't and I've never seen it here."

"Count your blessings," he said.

Tomás didn't so much seek my company as claim it as his due, and this highhanded attitude plus the sense that I had with him and his friends of being at the center of things gave him a certain fascination for me. I let myself believe there were strands of deeper feeling in him and that I might be able to separate these and work them into something satisfactory. "I think I rather approve of you," I said to him one night when we were lying in bed in the box room.

He folded his arms across his chest and said, "What's that supposed to mean?"

"To approve of is to be attracted to," I said, and he shook his head a few times.

"You think you rather approve of!"

I imagined him repeating the phrase to his friends, deploring the abuse of language. To me what I'd said was deplorable in its misrepresentation of feeling, for if I rather approved of Tomás I also rather disapproved of him. He wasn't serious enough for me. He wasn't sympathetic. He never said anything personal. He drank too much. I turned away from him and said, "Oh, go away."

"Now, Ann," he said, "you don't mean that. Here I was thinking I might spend the night."

Having roused him this far I found that I wasn't interested in going any further. "No, you won't," I said.

"I'd be up and off at dawn."

I reached out and put on the light. "You'll be up and off now."

He left with no great reluctance, and from then on I

began to see Tomás as a lost cause. Not through him would I get a grip on Ireland. That was something I had to work out on my own, and to this end I began making myself over. There was a shop on Duke Street that sold full skirts with borders that looked like designs from the *Book of Kells,* and I bought three of these plus a creamy pullover in the Aran style. I switched to tea instead of coffee for breakfast and I began eating fewer lamb chops and pork chops, more sausages and bacon, more potatoes. I acquired a taste for cabbage and a passion for brown soda bread and I stocked up on all this not at the little supermarket on Baggott Street but at Findlater's, a service grocery store where your money was placed in a cannister and sent along pulleys to the cashier's desk. One day as a Findlater's clerk was trying to cram my order into a thin paper bag, he muttered, "Get a shopping basket."

The one I bought was made of rushes from Slieve Bawn; Tomás disapproved. "What do you want that for?" he asked.

"For shopping," I said. "Everybody has one." But the baskets that Dublin girls all carried were made of willow and came from Woolworth's, as Tomás recognized.

"How much did it cost?" he asked.

I said, "None of your business."

"You can't tell me it cost less than ten shillings."

"What difference does it make to you?" I was a bit sick of Tomás, though after the night I put him out, the tables had turned, and the approval began to be all on his side. Now there was a tentative air to his skepticism, a note of uncertainty in his derision which gave it a plaintive quality. But I had no sympathy for him. He'd had none for me. One evening in early December when Theresa gave me the message that he'd rung and would ring again, I put my coat back on and went and had supper out; then I stopped off at the National Library. It was about half past eight. I'd never been there later than six and I found an entirely different place from the daytime room where I'd killed so much time so happily. No one seemed to be wool-gathering or even just reading for pleasure. I sat down in the first empty place, opened my book, and pretended to be engrossed. When I finally raised my eyes, I saw Tony Shields sitting at a desk in the alcove up front; he winked solemnly and lowered his gaze. I was wondering how soon I could leave without looking silly, when a shadow fell across my page, and I looked up again. Oona Ross was standing beside the desk. "Hello, Ann," she said, "or I should say goodbye."

I've spoken of Dublin as a small city where people continually run into their friends, but from the time I had supper at the mews till that evening at the National Library, Oona and I hadn't met. We kept different hours, but even so it was odd that our paths never crossed. Oona had her raincoat on, and her briefcase under one arm. "Are you leaving?" I asked, and she nodded. I said, "I'll come with you." I turned off the desk lamp and followed her to the check-in counter where she stopped for a word with the man on duty—Oona was on personal terms with everyone she ever met.

Out in the corridor she said to me, "We've been wondering where you were and how you were getting on," and I told her I hadn't wanted to be a pest, which was partly true. She said, "It's the people you want to see who think about pestering." I was doubly flattered—to have this value placed on my company and in a life that was clearly populous. "I suppose you found your flat," she said, and I confessed that I'd taken the room at Stella Philbin's. "I thought you would," she said. "And are you satisfied with it?"

"Reasonably."

"That's about all you can hope for with a bedsitter." We went out onto the library porch. "You wouldn't want to come by the mews for a cup of coffee?" she asked, and I said I'd love to. I put up my umbrella, but she didn't get under, and as we walked along, her raincoat was wide open. Oona was always oblivious to everything except what she had on her mind, and that evening it was the girls. "Daisy's much too young for all the responsibility I give her, but I don't know what else to do," she said. "I can't always be at home, and sometimes someone else has to take over." I asked how old Daisy was, and Oona told me, "Seventeen."

"At that age people want to be in charge anyway, don't they?"

Oona went right on. "Annabel's the complete opposite—lazy and wasteful and conceited and selfish. But poor Madeleine! The other day the dentist told me she's going to have bands on her teeth till she's twenty. She fell when she was five, and the second teeth grew in all wrong. She doesn't mind so much now, but think when she's twenty!"

"At home," I said, "even middle-aged people get their teeth straightened."

Oona would take the dimmest possible view before she risked consolation. "Madeleine was the one James worried most about. She was just born when he was stricken, and he knew that if he died the others would always have some trace of a father, but she'd be left with nothing."

I asked, "Was he sick long?"

"Three months," said Oona. "It was one of those awful things that wasn't exactly cancer but might as well have been. I went on hoping, but there wasn't any hope, and James knew. The nurses told me afterwards that he kept saying, 'What will Oona do? What'll become of Oona?' " By the time we reached the mews, its troubles had been so vividly impressed on me that it came as a welcome jolt, when I stepped inside, to find the place so calm and comfortable. Oona called, "Daisy!" and a distant hoot in response directed us up the spiral staircase. Madeline who was reading in bed ignored us, but Daisy came out into the hall. "Where's Annabel?" Oona asked.

"At Kathleen's studying," Daisy said. "Shall I make coffee?"

Of the three bedrooms, the largest was like a dormitory with trios of beds, desks, chairs, and wardrobes. Oona's room was small but it had a fireplace, and the embers of a perpetual turf fire gave the air there its sweet, burnt smell. She threw on another briquette and said, "Tell me everything you've been doing."

I began talking about Trinity and Proinsias O'Laoghaire and how I'd let him down. I described Dinah, and Tony, and I told how Mrs. Philbin had switched the bedspreads and palmed her old sheets and towels off on me. Daisy came upstairs with a tray and set it on the floor and poured the coffee. From time to time she smiled sorrowfully and said, "God help you," as I went on about the paraffin stove and the supposedly proper one, and about how I'd blown up the bathtub and now had to make an appointment with Theresa to use "Madam's."

"You know the story of Theresa, don't you?" Oona said. I didn't, and she told me, "She got pregnant when she was fifteen or sixteen, and Stella took her in. Now she's being 'good' to her."

Madeleine came into the room at this point. She had skin as fair as Snow White's, and her eyes were the palest blue—the blue, you'd have said, of pure intelligence. "Who are you talking about?" she asked.

"Be quiet," Daisy said. "Let Ann go on."

I told them then about Tomás—at least I told them something about him. The complete story of our evenings seemed inappropriate to the unconventional but highly respectable atmosphere of Oona Ross's family, and so I described him as someone from Cork I went out with quite a lot though in an unsatisfactory way. I sounded to myself much more affected by the situation than I believed I actually was; Oona had a way of drawing out your feelings though after she'd listened to you she often changed the subject. "Wait till you hear the latest," she suddenly said. "My mother wants to go and live with her sister in Castlebar."

"What she really wants is to live here," Daisy said and

she stood up and stretched and sat down again. "Aren't you lucky, Ann Clarke, to be all on your own."

"Not really," I said. "My responsibilities are just temporarily behind me."

Oona said, "My father once told me, 'Look after your mother, Oona, but look out for her, too.' " I asked what he was like, and she described him with a story. "One day when I was nineteen I was in the garden reading, and he came out to me all of a sudden and said, 'Get your things, Oona, I've a longing to see Connemara!' "

"My father didn't know I was alive," I said. But Oona had finished with fathers for the moment.

"We're having the most awful time with Tom Wynne. He's here all the time," she said, "and the girls are sick of him."

"He's always vocalizing," said Daisy. "It drives me mad."

Oona said, "Joe and Sally Wilson-Dunne say we must put a brake on him, but that's easier said than done. Joe and Sally are so clever and nice. I want you to meet them, Ann."

Back in New York, at lunch with the Driscolls, I'd dismissed the idea of my getting to know their friends, but in this similar situation I by no means jumped to the same conclusion. As I left the mews that evening, and Oona told me to come by whenever I felt like it, I said, "I will," and I meant it.

It was ten o'clock by the time I was back in the box room. I put on my bathrobe and was reading by the fire when Tony stopped by to ask, "What were you doing at the National Library?"

"Very little," I said. "Wasn't it obvious?"

"You certainly left in a hurry." He leaned an elbow on my stove. "What've you been up to, Ann? I knocked on your door once or twice, but you weren't in." He sounded hurt, and I felt a little guilty—we'd become friends, and then I'd gone and forgotten about him.

I said, "I've been on the town, Tony."

"Have you been to Mooney's yet? Mooney's pubs are the real Dublin."

"If it's all the same to you," I said, "I think I've had enough of the real Dublin." The open door was creating a draft in the room, and I turned up the collar of my bathrobe—a tailored viyella in a plaid that was mostly light blue.

Tony said, "You know, of all your getups, that little robe suits you better than anything."

"Thanks a lot," I said. "I put a fortune into Irish tweed, and now you tell me I look best in my bathrobe."

He smiled and said, "I'll make you a bargain—some evening I'll take you to Mooney's for a drink if you'll make me dinner on this so-called stove."

I said, "It's a deal."

In the home life of my family, stopping by had never played much part. Other people are leery of unhappiness, loathe to catch it out or maybe even catch it. By the same token unhappiness fosters a lack of spontaneity in those who live in its flickering light, and it was a couple of weeks before I returned to the mews. Then one night I went for a walk and ended up knocking at the wicket door. After two or three minutes of silence I knocked again, and after two or three more minutes I was about to leave; then Daisy came and peered out. "Oh, Ann, it's you," she said. "We were afraid it might be a fellow called Jim Larkin who drives us all mad."

Oona was sitting by the fire with Tom Wynne and a young man wearing glasses with steel frames. His nearsighted gaze and straight brown hair made me say to John Hogan, "You look exactly like—"

He put his hand up at me: "Don't finish that sentence."

But I did: "—James Joyce."

He said, "Are you a Joyce expert, Ann?"

"Nothing of the kind," I said.

"Those of your countrymen we get here in Ireland tend to be Joyceans with a vengeance." It was the kind of remark

I'd come to expect from Tomás and his friends, but John Hogan was so goodhumored that he could say such things without giving offense. He taught at University College Dublin but he had no scholarly ambitions or pretensions. "Someone has to do our research for us," he said. "God knows the Irish haven't the patience."

"Larkin would disagree with you about anyone having to do it," Oona said. She got up to put more turf on the fire and turned to me: "You'll meet Jim Larkin. He's a young librarian and a gifted poet but he's difficult."

"The fellow's a boor," said Tom.

"God help him," Oona said, "he probably has no choice. I doubt he's ever had enough attention—he has a kind of starved look."

"Which of us has had enough?" John said, sitting forward, clasping his hands between his knees. "Isn't it always too little love or too much?"

"Or bad timing," I said, thinking back to the man in New York—I'd always told myself that if I'd been a year or two older, in better command of myself, a little less dreamy, then things might have worked out between us, though at the moment I had no fault to find with a course of events that had led me to the warmth and companionship of Oona Ross's fire.

"James used to say, 'Love is a matter of timing, and loving is a matter of time,' " Oona said.

"The old business about falling in love, and managing to stay that way," said John.

"The one being an accident," she said, "and the other—well, surely the other's simply your life."

"It doesn't always work out that way," Tom Wynne said and then, with a stricken look: "I mean to say, people get fed up with each other, don't they?"

Oona faced up to the truth he'd accidentally hit on. "I'm no one to talk. James and I were never put to the test. We had all our happiness, and then it was all gone. Maybe in time we'd have ended up like most."

I don't think any of us believed that. I know I didn't. Oona struck me as someone who'd make a success of any unpromising circumstances. Hadn't she more than retrieved her widowhood, making that condition seem as interesting and as full of possibility as any other? At least that was how life at the mews looked to me, though I wondered if the girls appreciated it, for they were full of complaints. Daisy got up and said, "There's far too much talk in this house! Everyone's always going on about love or poetry!" And she stalked off to her room. In the slight uneasiness she left behind, it occurred to me that in a house where there were daughters, these young men were sitting and talking about love with the girls' mother. I thought of this again later that evening as I left with Tom Wynne and John Hogan. No sooner did the wicket door close behind us than things fell a little flat. Tom began going on about the Dublin opera season. "A month in the spring is no way near enough, and the company's tenth rate. Dublin should have its own opera company."

"It'd be wasted on me," said John. "What about you, Ann?"

Because I liked him and thought it better not to show my hand, I took the other side and said, "I like the opera."

"And which of them is the opera you like?" John asked dryly.

"Opera's the fullest expression of man's aesthetic capacity," Tom insisted.

John said, "Rubbish."

When we reached Fitzwilliam Square, a girl walked by and looked questioningly at my companions. "I always feel as if I'm cutting into their business," I said, and the two of them exchanged a glance that made me feel sharply contradicted. By the time we reached number twenty, I had the distinct impression that we were all just as glad to part company.

Seven   That fall and early winter were unremittingly wet, but they light my mind now with a radiance that outshines most beautiful weather anywhere that I remember. Every day by half past three or four, dusk set in; then how thrilling it was to be hurrying along those gleaming streets towards shelter and company—the smell of damp wool steaming in the heat of a turf fire, the sound of voices making speech a game or a contest or song. I think of that time as a season unto itself—raw as early spring, humid as a New York August, and with winter's own gray skies and sharp winds. No sooner were the Christmas decorations strung over Grafton Street than the garlands began to droop, and within a week half the lights had gone out, and the tinsel was all tangled.

One evening in early December I was sitting with Tomás and Liam at Nesbitt's. We were by ourselves at a small table, for it was a dull evening that seemed to reflect some general slackening in the atmosphere that I couldn't account for. "Where's everybody?" I asked.

"For one thing it's the end of the university term," said Liam. "People are all trying to catch up, or need I tell you that?"

I said, "I haven't been to class in three weeks."

"And here we've been led to believe Americans are such workers." Liam took my hand and kissed it. "No offense meant, dear Ann."

"None taken." The censure of Tomás and his friends was the price I paid for whatever benefits I derived from being one of their crowd, and though that mattered less and less to me, the situation had not yet run its course. There was besides, a small bonus of amusement and satisfaction that I got out of cashing in on the interval of faint remorse that sometimes followed a particularly obvious dig. "Let's go to Mooney's," I said.

"Where did you hear of Mooney's?" Tomás asked suspiciously.

Having no desire to make him jealous or even to let him think that was my intention, I explained who Tony Shields was, adding, "He told me Mooney's is the real Dublin."

"Mooney's is the lower depths," said Tomás. He got up and went over to the bar and bought one last round which there was barely time to finish when the barman announced that the place was closing. Tomás then went and bought the usual half dozen stout. Only when we were out on Grafton Street was I told, "We were thinking of going to your little place."

"All right," I said, "but we have to be—"

"I know, I know," said Tomás, "quiet."

In fact there was no great need for the stealth I'd instilled in him. Mrs. Philbin seemed hardly aware of my presence in her house, and whenever we met on the stairs or in the front hall she'd give me a distant smile and go on about her business. But with Tomás and Liam I felt the need to keep up appearances, lest they try and take advantage of the situation. They were such inveterate roisterers, and whatever they did created disorder of one kind or another. That night as Tomas skidded the car around to Fitzwilliam, the bottles of stout got shaken up, with the result that when we reached the box room, and Liam opened one, beer spurted out over him and onto the daybed. "Don't worry about it," I said, "that bedspread's the cheapest velvet."

"Your bedspread, my dear Ann, doesn't in the least concern me," said Liam. "It's my pants I care about."

"Won't the cleaner be able to get it out?"

"Ah," said Tomás, "the dry cleaner—America's answer to the confessional."

"Cleanliness is next to godliness," I said. "Remember?"
I gave Liam one of Mrs. Philbin's striped towels, and he
mopped himself off, but the accident put a damper on the
evening. The box room was a poor substitute for a pub,
anyway—too pretty to be suitable and too cramped to be
comfortable. They each finished a bottle of stout and smoked
two cigarettes apiece; then they left together. The next
morning I went to light the fire and discovered that my
matches were gone, the last box I had—Tomás or Liam had
made off with them! I put on my robe and stuck my head out
into the corridor. "You don't by any chance have some
matches?" I asked Dinah.

"Not a one," she said, "but I'll go ask Mr. Hughes."

"Never mind." I didn't like the idea of interrupting
someone's working day on such a dubious errand and I got
dressed and went to the shop at the corner. It was early to be
up and about after one of those nights. I felt woozy and back
in the box room I lit my fire and sat down to think things
over. In all probability Tomás and Liam hadn't known that
the matches they took were my last. But had they known
would they have stolen them anyway? It struck me as more
than likely. I remembered the first night we went out, when
Liam called home only to find that his wife had already taken
the receiver off the hook. What a wealth of angry experience
was in that gesture, and how could I have lost sight of it? By
telling myself Irish men behaved that way, and Irish women
overlooked it. But how spineless it was for me to have gone
along. I decided to turn over a new leaf : next semester I'd go
to my classes at Trinity and do the work, though the idea of
learning Irish had lost its great appeal thanks to the habit
Tomás and his friends had of using the language as a way to
exclude me. The thought of this filled me with resentment,
but as the bitter tide receded, I was left with the realization of
what at the moment I really had against him. He hadn't once
mentioned Christmas, and it appeared unlikely that he'd ask
me to spend the holidays with him.

"You'd be more than welcome to come home to London with me," Dinah said. Molly had dropped in, and we were having tea at the big desk on the landing. "It'd be just a family day—quiet, you know. Or perhaps you'd rather spend Christmas in Dublin. I expect I would in your shoes."

I said, "That's it. I hate to tear myself away for fear everything will change without my being here to see."

"Ann," said Molly, "Dublin hasn't changed in a hundred years and it's not likely to do so overnight."

"Let's leave it this way: if something better comes up, by all means grab it, but if not, come to the Kenyons'."

"Or if all else fails," Molly said, "come to the Corcorans' for an Irish family day—boisterous to the point of blasphemy. Rory says that when our clan gets together, you can hear us over in America."

A couple of days later Tony stopped by the box room. "Look here," he said, "if you've no plans for your holidays, you might want to come down to Cavan, though it'll be a rush job—down on Christmas Eve, back on Stephen's Day."

"What's Stephen's Day?" I asked him.

"December 26—what they call Boxing Day in England. Down the country it's a great time for visiting. Everybody lays on drink and cakes and such." Drink and cakes sounded to me like a deadly combination, and I told Tony that Dinah had asked me to go home with her. He said, "And the boyfriend might even come through, mightn't he? Well, just remember there's a place for you in Cavan."

Mrs. Philbin also asked about my plans one day as she was on her way out and I was on my way in. It was our longest conversation to date. "I've been meaning to ask where you're spending Christmas," she said, and I told her I wasn't sure. "But you'll have somewhere to go? I'm off to Scotland next week and I wouldn't like to leave you here by yourself." The guarded way she said this suggested it was the house she was thinking of—as if she pictured me racing from floor to floor opening drawers and closets, leaving the lights on, helping myself in the pantry. Though I'd have been more inclined to go through Stella Philbin's house raising the windows, letting fresh air into that stultified atmosphere.

I said, "If I don't see you before you leave—" and nothing was more likely, "—merry Christmas."

About a week later I'd washed my hair one evening and was drying it by the fire, having accepted in advance the split ends and the head cold with which I'd pay for this bit of playing the country lass. I heard the doorbell ring, and shortly afterwards Theresa came to tell me I had a visitor, adding in a whisper, "It's Mrs. Ross."

Reluctance to run into Stella Philbin had kept Oona from visiting me before this, and I found her standing by the front door, looking as guilty as Theresa. "I've only stopped by for a minute," she said. Somewhere in the house a door slammed, and she started. "Look," she said, "the girls and I were talking about Christmas, and I've got to tell you we won't be asking you over to us. Not that we wouldn't love having you. It's where you ought to be, but my mother's coming, and I can't face having anyone else."

Of the real possibilities I'd believed open to me, Christmas at the mews was the most attractive, but I said, "Don't give it a thought."

Her changed expression made her appear to be taking me literally, which was more or less the case. "Wait till you hear," she said, "we're having a party on Stephen's Day."

I'm a great one for holding out. You don't necessarily end up with exactly what you want but in place of settling early on for second, or third, or fourth choice you may get some fresh and desirable alternative like the one that came my way later that week in the form of a note from Beatrice Driscoll. She and Neil were back in Dublin, and she asked me to ring and make a date to meet them for lunch. I phoned at once and got Tricia who dropped the receiver; Beatrice picked it up and said, "Whoever you are, we beg your pardon." In New York her Irishness had struck me as forced, but now she spoke with an American accent that sounded just as artificial. "Where would you rather go," she asked, "Quo Vadis or Jammet's?" I didn't know where Quo Vadis was, but I could place Jammet's all right—that beautiful old restaurant on Nassau Street, across from Trinity, had become the symbol of my dissatisfaction with Tomás. I felt that he could have made an effort to take me there, and it galled me that the idea had never seemed to occur to him. I told Beatrice I hadn't been to either restaurant, and she said, "Haven't you been getting around?"

I said, "I'll tell you when I see you."

But Beatrice and Neil were indirectly responsible for my having met Tomás, and when I was sitting in *Quo Vadis* eating a wonderful *lasagne* at their expense, I watered down the story considerably, making it sound funnier than I felt to be the case. Beatrice kept nodding in a way she had that implied she'd been suspecting some such situation, though in fact Beatrice always seemed blind to the circumstances of other people's lives, being up to her eyes in the chief business of her own—keeping Neil happy and not neglecting Tricia in the process. It was Neil who sized things up that day. He put his arm around me and said, "What are you doing for Christmas, child?" I told him I didn't know yet, and he said, "Come to us."

"That's a marvelous idea," said Beatrice.

I didn't know whether or not to trust her but I had no such doubts about Neil. Beneath his air of simplicity could be seen something truly simple, fundamentally sad, and utterly reliable. "Come," he said, "an old friend of mine'll be there, too, and you'll round things off."

"Then that's settled," said Beatrice.

Eight Holidays away from home are uncon-//vincing. Like badly directed plays, they suggest the absence of a guiding spirit with a firm hand, and I took it as just another sign of this that the brief Christmas eve snowfall should have almost melted away by the time the sun rose—and then disappeared—on Christmas day. But children on their way to or from Mass were still able to scrape up wet handfuls to throw at each other. The streets were as busy as on any other weekday, and the people I passed appeared to be their weekday selves; if there were new knit hats and gloves, there weren't, as far as I could tell, diamond earrings or gold cufflinks; and no costly furs, no heady clash of perfumes and colognes. By early afternoon when I set off for dinner with Neil and Beatrice, calm—or a vacuum—had descended. Christmas at home could be empty enough, I reminded myself, but I'd expected the day to stand out in Dublin, and it struck me instead as particularly flat.

The building where the Driscolls lived was modern in the style of the 1940s, and when I saw their apartment I was glad I hadn't got one like it. Low ceilings and a stainless-steel kitchen gave the place an air of being modern without also being efficient, and though the central heating took the chill off the air, I'd rather have had a fire to sit by. I'd bought Tricia a cloth doll dressed in Irish homespun and as I gave it to her, I said to Neil and Beatrice, "I hope she doesn't have one."

Tricia opened the package and said, "I do have one. My dolly's name is Molly."

"They'll be twins, Trish," said Beatrice. "You can call the new one Dolly."

Tricia liked this idea and she began walking in circles chanting, "Molly, Dolly, Dolly, Molly."

I'd also brought a bottle of whiskey, and I presented it to Neil, saying, "I suppose it doesn't matter if you already have one of these."

"The more the merrier," he said.

"Now, now, none of that," said Beatrice and she took the bottle away from him.

Tricia began pulling on my hand, and I let myself be led over to the tree and shown her presents—storybooks and coloring books, sweaters and mittens, dolls and dolls' clothes, and a dose of educational toys. I was a little bored by the predictability of this spread and a little appalled by its lavishness, and Tricia sensed my disapproval. She became more and more self-conscious, more and more cranky; finally she began to cry, and at that point Neil's old friend, Desmond DeCourcy arrived. He was a scholarly man, an archaeologist, with thick gray hair and dark eyes full of intelligent shyness. "That sounds so solid," I said, "archaeologist." To be able to pin down the world and make it divulge its secrets—I envy that, but Desmond DeCourcy obviously thought I was just being polite.

"It's delicate work and hard work," he said, "digging."

"Sometime you should take Ann along to the site at Knowth, Des," said Beatrice.

As the day wore on I realized she had plans for Desmond DeCourcy and me. I then stopped calling him Mr. DeCourcy though I couldn't bring myself to say Desmond, much less Des. Not that I wasn't as susceptible to older men as young women are reputed to be, but Desmond DeCourcy wasn't an older man—he was an older boy, the kind of Irish bachelor who undoubtedly grew up without ever having much to do with girls. Beatrice probably reasoned that since he and Neil were contemporaries, Desmond DeCourcy was eligible, but Neil had a shaggy kind of sex appeal, and Desmond De-Courcy was devoid of any such thing. In his boyish and elderly way, he made his work sound as lifeless as the buildings where the results are put on display, and he talked about his dig all through the complete turkey dinner that it must have taken all Beatrice's ingenuity to assemble, given the limitations of the Dublin grocers. There was even cranberry jelly, lost like the rest of the meal on Desmond DeCourcy who ate absent-mindedly, talking on about passage graves and portal dolmens. My interest in all this had been waning for some time when he turned to me and said, "Actually you might like to visit the site. Or we might start with the museum. I'll ring you one day soon."

"Maybe after the new term begins, and I've got back into the swing of things." It was the first excuse that came into my head, and a pretty stupid one—obviously I'd have had more time during vacation than when school was in session (that is, if I'd actually been going to school), but no one picked this up.

"Who's your tutor at Trinity?" Neil asked me.

"As a matter of fact I was never assigned one. I suppose it was some sort of clerical error. I keep waiting for my day of reckoning though I don't know what I'm guilty of." Except, I said to myself, always taking the name of Trinity College in vain.

If holidays away from home are unconvincing, the particular holidays of a country you're visiting can be positively eerie. Though I didn't know what to make of Stephen's Day I felt obliged to observe it in some way and so I fixed myself bacon and eggs for breakfast and afterwards I sat down with my notebook but instead of adding to it I began reading back through what I'd already written. It started off prosaically: *The view at the end of Fitzwilliam is of mountains—that is, when you can see them. A certain kind of bad weather brings them out, and then sometimes—by no means always—you can discern the patterns of the planted fields, green and brown and gold. Most of the time it's only their outlines that show—like shadows, or low clouds.* Soon I was letting myself go:

When everything is beautiful, does nothing stand out? And is that what I love here? The stunning presence of ordinary beauty! And: *The Dublin gray has a beautiful sheen to it. All that rain, I suppose, though the effect seems to come from within.* By the end of November the entries had veered towards gossip: *Martin lives in Terenure where there's a Jewish community, so says Tomás. It seems to me Martin has to make an effort to be Jewish; being Irish comes more naturally to him.* And by December I'd turned a little sour: *Do Tomás and Liam ever speak to each other from the heart? Friendship is more than just hanging around together. To say nothing of love.*

I gave myself a Stephen's Day lunch of sausages; then I went for a walk. Fitzwilliam was deserted, and instead of heading towards Grafton Street I turned in the opposite direction and eventually found myself in Ballsbridge which was new to me and another world entirely from the shabby elegance of the Georgian squares. Walking along there I wondered how, with such a graceful standard close by for them to emulate, people could have gone in the direction of stolid, red-brick mediocrity. I got lost while I was about it, and it was three o'clock by the time I was on my own doorstep; there I met Tony, just returned from Cavan. "How was your Christmas?" he asked me.

"Fine," I said, "how was yours?"

"All right, I suppose." He looked dejected and when he said, "Come on upstairs—I brought a couple of bottles of lager back with me," I agreed. It was the first time I'd got a look at one of the top-floor flats, and it made me feel sorry for Tony, whose room was the classic garret, full of draughts and furnished with the barest of bare necessities. He opened the beer and poured mine into a jelly glass asking, "Well, how's the boy friend?" I said I had no idea, and he smiled and said, "Time for a change, is it?"

Time to change the subject, I thought. "What was it like at home, Tony?"

"Grand," he said, "grand." The woebegone look returned. "I hated coming back. This is no sort of life—

Maureen and the kids down there and me up in Dublin studying my arse off."

"When you have what you want you'll forget what it was like now," I assured him and wondered if that were true and went on, "You'll be the most important orthopedic surgeon in Dublin, setting all the best arms and legs."

He tilted the straight chair back as far as it would safely go and said, "You're a good girl, Ann."

"Tell that to Mrs. Philbin. I get the feeling she disapproves of me."

"What makes you say that?"

"Whenever I meet her she's very cool."

"Theresa tells me she's in London this week with the boy friend."

"Boy friend?" I shouldn't have been surprised. That was a logical conclusion to be drawn from the beautiful clothes and the socialite air. "Who is he?" I asked.

"Sir Jeremy Wolff, something grand in the way of a barrister from all accounts. He'll be over here next month. According to Theresa he always makes a visitation after the first of the year."

The beer on top of the fresh air and exercise was making me sleepy. "I can't finish this," I told Tony and I went back to the box room where I decided to take a nap; when I woke it was time to dress for Oona's.

I like parties and I don't like them. Meeting people is more fun when it's less organized, and though I love getting dressed up I hate deciding what to wear. Of my American clothes a gray flannel dress I'd bought two years before seemed both appropriate and warm enough, but when I tried it on I felt as if I were back in New York, going someplace after work. I took it off and tried my handwoven red skirt with a black cashmere sweater that had a wide neckline. It was a fairly strong understatement, and I also looked between continents, but that corresponded closely to my state of mind, and I wore the sweater and skirt to Oona's. When I got there, the wicket door was open, and noise and light were spilling out into the lane. Madeleine met me in the court-yard with the information, "I've had a glass of wine and I'm going to have another." As I followed her inside I knew with-out a doubt that I was going to have a good time and that I'd meet someone to replace Tomás in my affections—if it could in fact be said that his place was there. I'd no sooner got in the door when Beatrice grabbed me and whispered, "Get busy. There are loads of eligibles. How about the fellow with the drinks tray?" This was Tom Wynne.

"He's not my type," I said.

"Don't be choosy," said Beatrice and she put her hands on my shoulders and gave me a firm little push into the room. I kept on this course till a curly brown head turned, and I found myself facing Aideen Fitzgerald. My nemesis! She glared at me and turned her back again, and I made my way to the bar table. Fortified by a glass of wine, I was considering my next move when Oona brought a young man over.

"At last you meet!" she said, leaving me with Jim Larkin.

All I could remember about him was that no one liked him and I could see why. He had a terrible air of anxiety and a desperate desire to please. "You don't talk in the least like an American," he said, and I pretended to take this the wrong way. "What part are you from?" he asked awkwardly. When I told him, he cried, "Ah, New York—that must be a marvelous city!"

"It has its good points," I admitted.

"Do you like it here?" he asked, and I went on for a minute or two about Dublin; when I finished, he said, "We must do our best to keep you."

I saw John Hogan and waved, and he came over and said, "How's the Joyce scholar?"

"You've been around to Joyce's Dublin, have you?" asked Jim Larkin.

John said, "She has, of course, a dozen times, *Ulysses* in hand."

"You could use a little respect for your heritage, John Hogan," I said.

The life in this conversation was between the two of us. Jim Larkin soon gave up and drifted off, but John and I had played ourselves off against him, and he left a gap. I was just as glad when Beatrice joined us with someone she introduced as "Peter Bruce, a compatriot, Ann." In New York or Boston or Washington I might have approved of the gray flannel, the pink shirt, the hornrimmed glasses, but Dublin had accustomed me to disreputable-looking men, and Peter Bruce struck me as too smooth.

"Bea tells me you're studying with Proinsias," he said. "I'm a great admirer of his."

I said, "So am I but I'm afraid it's not mutual."

"That's difficult to believe."

"Well, it's true," I said.

"What else are you doing at Trinity?"

"It's hard to say."

"You're not matriculated then?"

"I may not even be fully registered."

It was the kind of cross-purposes that doesn't mesh, and eventually I said I thought I'd get another glass of wine. By that time John had evaporated, but I was glad to have a chance to survey the crowd. It was an agreeable conglomeration—women who might have stepped out of the houses I'd seen that afternoon in Ballsbridge, and others dressed in the eccentric and colorful style I associate with women who paint. There were a couple of girls like Aideen Fitzgerald, aggressively student in manner; and a few well-dressed, well-bred debutante types. All the men looked prosperous, even those who also looked artistic—that is to say those whose coats and trousers didn't match and whose minds appeared to be elsewhere. And as Beatrice had said, several of them seemed distinctly eligible. I was trying to decide which of them was my best prospect, when someone spoke to me: "Do you like this party?" I turned and got the impression that he'd been watching me for a few minutes though I hadn't noticed him. Michael Flynn wasn't someone who stood out in a crowd—his manner was subdued, though his attention, when he gave it, was disconcertingly close. He rephrased the question, "Would you say this is a good party?" and I backed off a little.

"Excellent," I said. "Brilliant, from what I've seen of Dublin parties."

"What sort of parties?"

"The ones full of native speakers."

"Tell me what they're like."

"Aren't you Irish?" I wasn't perfectly sure, and there was a reason why.

"Yes, but I'm a little out of touch. I'm just back from a year in Finland," and he launched forth. "That's supposed to be the freest society in the world, and yet Scandinavians are dull and repressed, they have one of the highest rates of drunkenness, and their rates of insanity and suicide are comparable. It's a relief to be back in Dublin where people at least know how to drink and to keep their wits about them."

I said, "I wonder."

"I'm settling in out at Churchtown. I've a little place in the fields there. Where do you live?" When I told him, he asked if he could see me home, but I said I wasn't ready to leave. "When you are?" he persisted, and I agreed to leave with him, whereupon he moved off again. I was on my own till a woman in a hat with a long feather approached me and said, "I want you to meet my daughter. She's going out to America this summer." I set off after her, but halfway across the room I got sidetracked by a fellow with a European accent who told me he was with the Belgian Embassy and asked what I did.

"Practically nothing," I said in all honesty.

"You are droll, you Irish," he said with a puzzled smile, and I told him I wasn't Irish. "But your eyes, your coloring!"

"Irish-American," I said.

"Is there such a difference?"

I was about to enlighten him, but Tom Wynne began clapping for attention and then announced that he'd been asked to sing. Though he kept going flat, I was moved by his rendition of "She Is Far from the Land," that extravagant lament in the Irish tradition of tragic death and eternal fidelity. During "The Croppy Boy" people began talking again, and by "Breathe Not His Name," Tom was singing to himself. John Hogan came up to me and said, "You left me in the lurch, Ann."

"You left me," I corrected him.

"Can I give you a lift?" he asked. "I have the car outside."

I wished I hadn't had to say, "Some else asked me. I suppose he was serious." I looked around and located Michael Flynn on the other side of the room, talking to Annabel who was laughing, though I'd have said Michael meant every word. I wondered if it'd be worth the trouble to try and sneak off without him, but John took the matter as settled.

Soon after this, as though he'd been keeping an eye out, Michael came over and asked, "Will we go now?"

I went and found Oona and said goodnight. She pressed my arm and said, "Come by tomorrow. We'll have a great old chat."

When I joined Michael in the lane, he began talking about the party again, telling me what was wrong with it. This time I said, "I thought it was a wonderful party."

"But not typical."

I said, "I wouldn't know about that."

"Your Irish-speaking friends must be typical," he reminded me.

"But not exactly wonderful." We crossed Baggot Street to Fitzwilliam where a couple of prostitutes walked by. "Business as usual," I said.

"Does it bother you?"

"Not really." But the truth was, those women had begun to disturb me with their perpetual sauntering, like an unanswerable question going around and around at the back of my mind.

"How do you happen to know Oona?" Michael said.

I told him that Neil had introduced us, and he asked how well I knew Neil. It was less a conversation than an interrogation. I said, "Why do you ask?"

"Just curious. And do you know Oona well?" he went on. I asked how well he knew her, and he said, "Hardly at all. I wouldn't have been there tonight if I hadn't run into her last week on Grafton Street."

But for that chance meeting I might have been sitting in John Hogan's car which would have suited me better. When we got to my door, Michael Flynn took out a pocket notebook and carefully wrote down the address and asked if I had a telephone. I gave him Mr. Hughes's number; then he asked where I spent most of my time. That struck me as efficiency carried too far and misguided in the first place. To put him off the track I told him, "The National Library," and he wrote it down, wrote out his own address and phone number, tore the page from the notebook, and handed it to me:

Small House
Hawthorn Park
Churchtown

I said, "It's like a little poem."

"It's a pretty place," he said. "You'll like it there."

I thought, That remains to be seen. But all the same, this fullblown attention made an impression on me—someone you don't have to cultivate is a nice change.

Parties and accidents have in common that both invite postmortems, but even in the reconstruction events don't always add up, and I got a slightly different, less coherent impression of that party the next day, talking it over with

Oona and the girls. "Well," she said, "you missed out on Jim Larkin. He left with Aideen Fitzgerald."

"That puts him in an entirely different light," I said.

"She's an old friend of John Hogan's."

I said, "That puts *him* in a different light."

Oona told me, "One day he came to me with a story about a girl he knew who was going around with an alcoholic and he asked would I see her. I don't think there ever was much between John and Aideen except talk. What did you think of Larkin?" I couldn't pretend that he'd appealed to me. "He's brilliant," said Oona, "but instead of shining he burns."

"Which man was your favorite?" asked Madeleine. "Mine was Peter Bruce."

Oona said he'd asked if I were on the phone, and I was pleased rather than not—for someone basically attractive to be interested in you can sometimes be enough for you to begin to return the interest, and it was in more or less this spirit that I asked about Michael Flynn. Oona said, "A couple of years ago he was going round with Aideen."

"Dublin *is* a small city." The truth of this was at last getting through to me.

"Sometimes I used to meet her for tea," said Oona. "She's intelligent but unstable. Once she asked if she could come to the farm with a fellow she was trying to impress. She and Michael rode down on their bikes and went back the same evening."

"He talked too much," Daisy complained.

"And according to Aideen he used to belong to *Opus Dei*," Oona said.

"That sounds innocent enough." But with ominous overtones, I thought. "What is it?"

"A kind of lay religious order," said Oona. "They don't live in communities but they practise celibacy."

"That's odd all right." But I wasn't exactly put off, for it was oddness that presupposed hidden depths in the flat individual who'd seen me home.

Daisy said, "I wonder how you go about practising celibacy. Three hours a day like the piano?"

"I saw you talking to Léon, Ann. Isn't he the cruelest bore?" said Annabel.

"Who's Léon?" I asked, and she told me that was the name of the Belgian. "All clothes," I said.

We sat around drinking tea and eating biscuits for most of the afternoon. At half past five when I got home, Theresa intercepted me in the hall. She was beside herself: "Mr. O'Domhnaill's been ringing all afternoon, Miss Clarke, and he says he'll keep on ringing. Or he might come by, so he said."

I didn't want to see Tomás, and fifteen minutes later when the phone rang, I didn't answer it. Half an hour went by, and I'd begun to relax; then I heard the doorbell. I went over and stood listening by the box-room door. It was Tomás; he and Theresa were coming upstairs. I turned off the light and moved over to the bed and sat there holding my breath during the conversation that took place at my door.

"Maybe she stepped out for a minute," said Theresa.

"But you're after telling me she's after coming in!" Tomás tried the door and said, "I'll just wait in there till she's back."

"I don't know, Mr. O'Domhnaill."

Tomás assured her it'd be all right and came into the box room. As if I'd been asleep and were waking I turned on the desk lamp and stretched my arms. "Where were you?" he asked. "I've been ringing all afternoon." He took off his coat and threw it on the bed.

I said, "How was your Christmas?"

"I stayed in Cork. I was working." He sneezed twice. "And got a bloody awful cold for my trouble." I offered him some aspirin, but he said, "What I want is your razor." When he found it in the cabinet over the basin, he took off his tie, rolled up his shirtsleeves, and began splashing and soaping his face with a nonchalant air that was partly genuine and partly bluff—know the box room he certainly did but he'd never before made an effort to feel at home there and he didn't quite pull it off. "I told Liam we'd meet him at Nesbitt's at half six," he said.

"Shouldn't you stay in with that cold? Besides," I said, "I don't really feel like going out."

Tomás dried his face and said, "What would become of us all if we only did what we felt like?"

"You make it sound as if it's a duty to go out drinking."

"In a way it is," he said.

And in a way I agreed with him. If you don't get around and meet people and enjoy yourself when you can, how do you get your life arranged? And once it's arranged, how do you keep it from going stale except in the course of what's called social life, or a good time. Neither is the right description for the various ways and means to that enduring end—getting to know people, making them like or love you, learning to handle yourself in the situations you walk or are thrown into. All that is just as serious as holding a job, and being civic-minded, and eating properly, and having your teeth looked after, and the rest of what's covered by expressions like, "Come down to earth" and "Keep you feet on the ground."

Tomás rinsed my razor and left it to dry. "Get your coat, Ann."

"All right," I said, "but I'm not staying out late and I'm only going to Nesbitt's."

But there was no sign of Liam there, and of course we went on to Neary's where we found him sitting at the bar talking to a fellow who had bushy blond hair and wore a shapeless suit of fuzzy tweed that looked homespun and horribly expensive. He had a vague expression and was drunk, but Liam's introduction had a note of respect instead of the usual mock courtesy. "Colin is one of the Ashby-Smyths from County Down."

"I met a Gavin Ashby-Croft some years ago," Tomás said and he took out his handkerchief and blew his nose.

"Colin's waiting for Larry Robinson who just got out of

jail," Liam told us.

"Robinson punched a guard," said Colin. "Seamus Duffy put up the bail, but for some reason or other Robby's raging at Duffy."

It sounded like juvenile behavior to me, and I leaned over and said as much to Tomás. "Don't start," he warned me. At this point a seedy-looking man entered the bar; this was Larry Robinson. His clothes were filthy, and he had shifty eyes, but he was given a hero's welcome and asked to relate his experiences. Midway in the story he leered at me and asked, "Who's the girl?"

"Go on, Robby," Colin said, "tell us what Duffy did."

"Made a speech. Gets up and says, 'Ireland's a backward land full of obsolete laws and degenerate law officers. It's time,' says he, 'that we corrected the situation.' I was afraid of my life they'd refuse bail."

Colin ran a hand through his bushy hair and said, "Look, let's clear out of here and go back to my flat."

It was an hour to closing time, but Liam said, "Let me just finish my pint."

"Where is this flat?" I asked Tomás.

"I don't know," he whispered, "but it'll be lavish. He's rich, Colin is."

"I'm not in the mood for one of those parties." But I didn't put up any resistance. The idea of seeing a luxurious Dublin flat appealed to me, and I wasn't disappointed by Colin Smyth's four sumptuous rooms full of expensive furniture. The walls were covered with red flock paper, and there were beautiful carpets, beautiful pictures.

Tomás stretched out at once on the George II sofa, saying, "I'm half dead. I drove up from Cork at six this morning—and with this cold."

I said, "You should be home in bed."

"I should be in Tananarive," he said, "which for your information is the capital of Madagascar where there's sun three hundred and fifty days of the year."

Liam said, "Well, Colin, what can you offer us to eat?"

"I'm afraid not a thing. Shall I go out?"

"Yes, dear boy," Liam said, "run over to Paris for some pâté."

"Seriously—I know a shop that stays open till midnight and sells cooked chickens and things."

Liam's deferential air had turned truculently and perhaps enviously casual. "Go along then," he said, and before Colin was out the door, Liam had sat down with the telephone book and started ringing pubs, asking for people and telling them to come around.

"Should he do that?" I asked.

Tomás said, "Don't be so bloody proper."

The regulars began arriving, plus another crowd, none of whom I recognized, all of them vaguely English-looking, well-dressed and affable, with names like Simon and Cyril. There was also a piper who set up shop in the kitchen, and by the time Colin returned, his flat was full of people trying to talk over the music. "I wonder will this be enough," he said, taking chickens and eggs and cheeses from his shopping basket. He was so agreeable and so silly that the use being made of him would have been shocking had he not happily gone along. I turned to Tomás and said, "What a fool."

"Get hold of yourself," said Tomás.

I left him and went wandering about, looking at the pictures. In front of a charcoal drawing of some rather forbidding, fair-haired woman I met Martin Brodie. "What in heaven's name are we doing here?" I asked him.

"You're here because you're with Tomás," he said. "I have no excuse except that I come when I'm called."

I said, "I don't believe that."

"But you must, it's the truth."

I realized that it probably was, that Martin and I were less alike than I'd let myself imagine, and I wasn't sorry when the seedy-looking Larry Robinson came over and began a reprise of his grievances. "What do you make of that fellow Duffy? Gets me out of jail and then gives a speech about it!"

I said, "It seems to me you got off easy."

"You don't know what easy is if you think it's easy being in jail at all."

"I didn't say being in jail was easy," I pointed out, but he ignored this.

"Then along comes a fellow gives a speech that nearly gets you thirty days more. By God I don't call that easy!" He began running his hand up and down my arm. I moved away, but he came after me and kept on stroking my arm.

"Would you mind not doing that?" I said.

"You're a good-looking girl. Isn't she a good-looking girl, Victor?" he asked the man next to him.

"Of a sort, of a sort," Victor said.

I left them and went looking for Tomás and found him in the bedroom eating a leg of chicken. I told him I wanted to leave, and he asked, "Aren't you enjoying yourself?"

There was in this question a deliberate and unlikeable obtuseness that infuriated me. "Of course I'm not enjoying myself, and neither are you. You rush around and drink yourself stupid and tell yourself you're having fun. Well, let me tell you you're mistaken."

He took a bite that stripped the chicken bone clean; then he put it down and calmly said, "We'll leave so, if you like, Ann."

In the time it took me to get my coat he'd started a conversation with one of the Simons or Cyrils but he broke it off as soon as I appeared. "Where in heaven's name are we?" I asked when we were outside. Driving to Colin's we'd taken a back-street route which had made the flat seem at some distance from Grafton Street, but it proved to be near the center of town and only a block or two from Fitzwilliam. Tomás and I made this short drive in silence till we reached number twenty, where he said, "I'll see you in."

"That's not necessary," I said, but he got out and

followed me to the door. I put my key in the lock, turned to him and said, "Good night, Tomás." I meant, "Goodbye." I'd had enough of him and his friends and what's more I felt no further need of them. Tomás understood this, and when I stepped inside and started to close the door, he put his shoulder to it. I pushed from my side, but he was too strong for me. "Oh, all right, come in," I said, "if you must." We went quickly and quietly upstairs to the box room where I turned on all the lights and lit the fire.

"It's a nice little room," Tomás said as he sat down on the daybed. "Nice and cozy."

I said, "When did you change your mind?"

"Now, Ann, don't be difficult."

"I'm not." In fact I was nervous. I wished I hadn't had to let him in and I wondered how soon I could get rid of him.

"You're being very difficult." He got up and came over to me, but I stepped aside. "In fact, you're being bloody unpleasant." He tried to kiss me. I kept twisting away, but he held on, backing me towards the bed. It entered my head that we were bordering on rape, but I didn't really believe it and I must have been trying to infect him with my own incredulous dismay when I said, "You can't be doing this!"

"Can't I?"

"Why don't you be yourself!" This appeal to the basically decent Tomás was a waste of breath, for Tomás the rake was in full command. He pushed me down on the bed and fell on top of me. As he began fooling with my clothes, I swung my head, giving him a knock on the chin that made him bite hard on his tongue. "Jesus!" he cried, loosening his grip. I jumped up and went over to the fireplace, but he came after me. I wondered whether I'd have to hit him and with what—Mrs. Philbin hadn't furnished the box room with a view to scenes of frustrated passion, and the closest thing to a weapon was the desk lamp. Beside it was a letter from my sister that had come the day before, and this gave me an idea. "You're mean to do this," I said, "now when things are awful for me."

The protest was so feeble and the grounds so obscure that it caught him up. "What things?"

"Family things," I began to improvise. "I just got word that my father's walked out on my mother."

The color at once left Tomás's face, and it took on a mottled look. "Walked out?" he said.

The lie had more than a grain of truth; three times in the past my father in fact went to live with his sister, and as I stood there facing Tomás, this reality was fresh in my mind. It's fresh to me still—the shame of those days when Barbara and I discovered that the life we were living was a counterfeit, and that in the life ahead we would be obliged to try and impersonate people whose belief in human happiness had been less thoroughly undermined.

Tomás took out his handkerchief and wiped his nose. The air of indifference that put me off all along had vanished. Instead he had the eager look of someone who has suddenly come to his senses and wishes to mend his ways. "Jesus," he said, "I didn't know."

"You didn't ask!"

He put his handkerchief back in his pocket and left his hand there; in this pose he put me more than ever in mind of someone in a family tintype—ironically, in view of what he said next. "My own father deserted us—wife and six children under twelve. He left one day and never was heard from again."

"Why didn't you ever tell me?" I thought of all the evenings we'd spent together and all the talk there'd been—of Irish poets and poetry, Irish music, Irish culture, Irish tradition. I'd much rather have listened to his personal history and have had him listen to mine.

"Well," he said, "I've told you now, haven't I?"

"You should have done it sooner!"

Tomás knew that, wanted to believe otherwise, and got

to his feet. I was afraid he might attack me again and so I didn't mind when he gave me a kiss on the cheek, though the sympathy and understanding he invested in it were wasted on me. "Good night, Tomás," I said firmly, and he backed off, his little blue eyes dark with the knowledge that whatever he was offering had come too late.

The letter from my sister that I'd used to get rid of Tomás made no reference to either of my parents. It was all about an idea of Barbara's:

> . . . I'd come over the week after Easter. We could hire a car and drive around or stay in Dublin. It seems like years, not just four months. . . .

My sister and I are physically alike, and that serves to disguise and probably compound our few but important differences. Barbara has more confidence than I do—that much at least the older child can make of first place—but she'd probably deny this because she knows herself less well than I know her, much less well than I know myself. Though she cries easily she's not truly in touch with the feelings that bring on those tears that get me so riled. Ironically, always having to measure up to her has taught me to be tough—not an unqualified asset, I've learned. A lot of the time I act more concerned or interested than I feel, which can lead people to believe I'm nicer than Barbara, though usually when we two are together our differences get lost in the similarity. In fact, my features are smaller and my expression soberer than Barbara's, but people are generally slow to spot this, with the result that I'm forever making some point or stating some position in order to avoid the confusion of my sister with me. The effect of always having to demonstrate what I am is that I end up less free to be it. After I got her letter this began preying on my mind, and one afternoon I brought the subject up with Dinah.

"Growing up, I longed for a sister," she said.

"The real thing's a mixed blessing."

"I invented one and called her Cynthia. She went everywhere with me."

"You get sick of that."

"Perhaps," said Dinah.

I wasn't getting through to her, and the desire to unburden myself continued to build up till with this in mind I went over to the mews later that week. When I knocked on the wicket door, it swung open. I looked inside and called, "Hello!" but there was no answer, and I went on into the courtyard and found the storm door ajar, so I stuck my head inside. It was dusk, and when my eyes adjusted to the indoor light, or the lack of it, I noticed someone sitting facing the fire, an old woman who half turned and called, "Is that you, Oona?"

I went to her and said, "You must be Oona's mother. I'm Ann Clarke."

"Our friend from New York!" I liked this description and I wished I could also have liked Mrs. Kehoe, but that proved impossible. "Oona's gone off to the shop for biscuits," she said. "Here we were about to have our tea, and not a biscuit in the house. I can't think what's taken her so long. She's gone twenty minutes when she shouldn't have been two."

"I'll keep you company," I said.

Her eyes flooded with the accumulated doubt and infirmity of her great age—which was near ninety—but she spoke in a girlish voice. "Tell me about yourself. Oona's mentioned you but she hasn't told me a thing about you." I said I was studying at Trinity, and she cried, "Ah, when James died, Oona could have taught at university but of course she wouldn't. I've always thought she'd be far better off teaching than the way she is now, but no one can tell Oona anything." A car door slammed nearby, and a minute later Oona herself was at the wicket door. "Oona's always acted as she pleased," said Mrs. Kehoe, "though I don't know what good it's ever done her."

"That's not true!" Oona came in crying. "You know it's

not true, mother! Hello Ann, you're just in time for tea. Help me get the tray." I followed Oona into the kitchen where she laid the paper bag of biscuits on the table and put her face in her hands; I thought she was crying, but when she looked up, her eyes were dry and full of angry despair. "She's driving me mad," she said.

"Don't say anything when we go back. I'll do the talking," I offered.

But no one could have held out against Mrs. Kehoe's baiting. Handed a plate of chocolate biscuits, she said, "You didn't get any plain ones, did you, Oona? The chocolate always sticks to the roof of my mouth. I don't suppose you remembered."

I said, "I've developed a craving for chocolate biscuits."

"You have lovely ones in America," Mrs. Kehoe reminded me. "When I visited my sister in Philadelphia I used to love the cream sandwiches and the mallow biscuits. Oona couldn't get enough of those mallows the time I brought her out with me. She was just Madeleine's age." Mrs. Kehoe looked around and asked, "Where are the girls? Ah well, I don't suppose they can be expected to wait and see their grandmother."

Oona said, "They're over to the flat every couple of days!"

"But I don't see them here. Of course, I'm here so seldom." It was such a basic, the lesson Mrs. Kehoe hadn't learned: you can't make people listen to you just by wanting them to, much less will wanting be enough to make anyone love you and do what you ask.

Finally Oona said, "Look, mother, it's getting late, and I'm going to drive you home. Will you come along, Ann?"

Mrs. Kehoe had been set up in a flat that was like the Driscolls'—modern in the style of the 1940s. The rooms had low ceilings and built-in radiators, but here there was also a fireplace though the fire that was laid in Mrs. Kehoe's living room looked as if it were never lit. "Sit for a minute," she begged.

Oona said, "You know I've got to get to the library."

"Will you be by tomorrow?"

"I'll send one of the girls."

"What time?"

"Late afternoon."

"Not too late!"

We got out the front door, but she kept calling after us till we were back in the car. "You wouldn't go over every so often and see her?" Oona asked as we drove off. "I can't always do it myself. She takes my life and scrambles it into something of her own."

"So does my sister," I said. "In a different way though. She's coming over to visit me in April."

"Is she like you?"

"That's a long story."

"Don't worry," Oona said, "when the time comes we'll help you out."

Nine At the beginning of February a real guest turned up at number twenty. "Stella's heart-throb," Dinah called him.

Once or twice I passed Sir Jeremy Wolff on the stairs, and each time he stopped and bowed. He was a polished old gent, polished in manner and in appearance: tall and sleek with white hair and a neat white moustache that emphasized his high color. He dressed in conservative gray with sporty touches—fawn-colored vest, a Paisley handkerchief in his breast pocket, a carnation in his lapel. One afternoon I met him and Mrs. Philbin together, and in the manner of someone deciding to turn misfortune to advantage, she said,

"Are you free this evening? I'm having friends in for drinks and I like my guests to join me."

I don't know why I assumed that Dinah would be included among the "guests," but that afternoon I said to her, "Let's go together tonight." She asked where, and I felt awkward having to tell her.

"I'm not one of the chosen," she said. "Though I've been to one or two of Mrs. Philbin's parties, and they're quite nice."

Dinah had to work late that evening and she was still at her desk when people started arriving. "Why am I going to this?" I complained.

"Stop by the flat afterwards, if you feel like it," she said. "Molly's coming round."

The black sweater and red skirt I'd worn to Oona's had turned out to be so successful that I was wearing it again, but when I walked into the lounge I felt as if I'd deliberately set myself up as a contrast to the middle-aged men and women standing around there in small, sedate groups. I looked for Tony, and Lady Colby's son, but I seemed to be the only boarder present. Mrs. Philbin was posed with her elbow on the mantelpiece, and when our eyes met, she smiled coldly as if she were willing me to turn around and walk out, which I might have done but for Theresa who came over with the champagne, lifting her chin at me as if to say, "Stand your ground." I began sipping my drink, feeling ill at ease, picking up a bit of the conversation nearest me.

"Kathleen and Stan have entered Eagle Eye in the Spring Show," said a tall woman.

"Why Eagle Eye's no better than a dray horse!" another woman said. "I thought Stan was grooming Falstaff for the Show."

I stepped into the group with a question. "What's the Spring Show?"

Everyone looked pained. "At the Royal Dublin Society," said one of the men, "an agricultural event, really." They continued their conversation, and I latched onto another group where the talk was more intelligible to me but no more interesting.

"Daphne's Mercedes arrived last week."

"I thought she was buying a Citroen."

"At the last minute they couldn't deliver in the color she wanted."

I hadn't crossed the Atlantic to stand around listening to conversation about cars and I moved off again. This brought me alongside Sir Jeremy who said, "You look a bit confused. And here I thought Americans always landed on their feet."

"Which Americans?" I asked, and he laughed.

"Quite right. Stupid generalization. Tell me what sort you are—no, let me tell you. Headstrong girl of good family, a little bored with life, looking for a bit of fun."

Acting out a character that's imposed usually seems to me kinder and is certainly less bother than trying to impose your own character with people who don't really matter to you, but I was sufficiently out of place in that room to want to explain myself and I was about to when I happened to catch Mrs. Philbin's eye. She had an expression of the most intense dislike I've ever seen in a look directed at me. I had no special desire to be in my landlady's good graces but I didn't especially desire to be out of them either and I said to Sir Jeremy, "I've got to go."

The low fire of aging lust lit his mind and momentarily made his handsome face look sad and coarse. "Meeting your young man, are you?"

The easiest thing to say was "Yes," but in fact I hadn't anything to do; though it was two weeks since Oona's party, nothing had developed out of it. Back in September, having evenings to myself made me feel more intensely the sensation, and thus the benefit, of being abroad, but since then there'd been Tomás. However unsatisfactory he'd been, without him life seemed dull, and when I got back to the box room I changed my clothes and went over to Dinah's. She and Molly were having baked beans on toast; she went to fix some for me, and Molly said, "How was the big bash?"

"Awful," I said. "I don't know why I was invited, unless Mrs. Philbin felt she had to when she ran into me."

Molly said, "More likely she was embarrassed in front of her beau about setting the box room. She probably wanted to make it seem as if she'd only done it because you'd got on like a house on fire."

"She wasn't very convincing this evening," I said.

"Or then again," said Molly, "maybe she was simply trying to act your age."

Something along those lines had already occurred to me. I said, "You don't suppose that all this time she's been expecting me to make friends with her?"

Molly said, "Oh brother!"

"She's so temperamental," said Dinah. "You wouldn't know what was going on inside that head of hers."

We left it at that, but I began to feel as if I'd been expected, might be expected still, to exert myself in Stella Philbin's direction. I had no such desire—I was renting a room in her house, I reminded myself, not visiting there. "Well, anyway," I said, "it was a really terrible party."

"What could you expect?"

"Molly, that's unkind," said Dinah.

"Oh, dry up, Di." Molly lit a cigarette and asked, "What time is it?"

I said, "Half past ten."

"Rory's coming by," Dinah told me. "That's why she's in such a state."

I'd begun to think Molly had invented this Rory, but the fellow who arrived shortly after eleven was no phantom. Tall, black-haired, blue-eyed, he was a good example of a common Dublin type, the Adonis with a simple nature and an old-fashioned, bashful disposition. "Ah now, Molly," he kept saying, as she blustered on about how wet he'd got.

"Riding around on the motorbike in this rain! You'll get pneumonia one of these days and then where'll you be?"

"In hospital for a well-deserved rest," said Rory. "You can steal by with the odd pint."

"You mean the odd punch," Molly said.

"Pint or punch, so long as I wet my whistle."

Sitting there listening to them I envied Molly, not for Rory himself but for whatever it was in her that would like someone so wholesome.

The men who appeal to me are invariably complicated, cranky, unsettled and unsettling—that summed up my second impression of Michael Flynn who turned up at the National Library the following week. Rain had plastered his hair to his head, and for a second or two I didn't recognize the face looking at me over the green glass shade of the desk lamp. "Can you step outside?" he whispered. I followed him from the reading room, and as the doors swung shut behind us, he asked, "Will you come out with me?"

The perfect seriousness with which he put this cryptic question made me ask, "Where?" as if he were suggesting we fly to Paris.

"I thought we'd take a walk," he said.

"In this rain?"

"Does it bother you?"

"I suppose not." I went back inside for my coat, my books, my umbrella; when I joined him again, he apologized.

"I shouldn't have interrupted your work. I'd kill anyone who did that to me." I realized I didn't know what sort of work he did and I asked about it. He said, "I'm writing a book about modern Ireland."

"Isn't that a contradiction in terms?"

"On the contrary. There's no real progress that doesn't bring the whole past along with it—otherwise things eventually fall apart. That'll never happen here. The Irish people are too sure of themselves."

I said, "I know what you mean."

"That sounds like the voice of bitter experience."

"I wouldn't exactly say bitter."

At the top of Kildare Street we crossed over into the Green. It was deserted in the rain, and you could better see the grand design—paths winding into one another and culminating in the large circular bed of grass, flowerless at that time of year, the fountains shut off. I said, "This is how I imagined the whole of Ireland to be."

"Verdant?"

"And civilized."

"It's better than that—a real 'Garden of Delights.' Do you know the picture?" I told him I didn't. "By Hieronymous Bosch, a sixteenth-century Flemish painter," he said. "I've a book about his work that might interest you."

We stood on the bridge to watch the ducks paddle about, splashing and quarreling with each other. "What made you come to Ireland?" he asked. "The adventure of it?"

I shook my head. "I'm more the conventional than the adventurous type." Meaning this to be contradicted I minded when instead he agreed.

"Don't be offended. It's good to be conventional," he said.

But to the extent that I use the conventions as camouflage, the description was inaccurate, and this bothered me. I said, "You don't seem particularly Irish."

"Oh?"

I'd struck a sore spot and succeeded in provoking him, showing that I was able to hold my own. I could afford to back down a bit. "You seem more European."

"Actually," he said, "I was born in the North, in Armagh." This was just before the Provisional I.R.A. surfaced along with the Ulster Defense League, before Falls Road and Shankill impressed the mentality and the geography of Northern Ireland on the rest of the world. Armagh might have been another Cork as far as I knew then. He said, "When I was a child, my mother and father came here to make their way and left me up there with my grandparents."

"I suppose it was a last resort," I said, since my experience has been that people don't really want you to enter into their family grievances. Michael proved an exception.

"Not at all—it was pure avarice. I was ten before they got round to sending for me. Eventually I moved out and went to live with my aunt."

He presented this factually not angrily but not, either, as if he'd reconciled himself to the story however often he told it—and I got the impression that he did so at the drop of a hat. Or maybe it was just the rain getting through to me, making me hard on him. "Look," I said, "it's pouring—why don't you come back to the flat, and we'll have tea."

"Not today." He stuck his hands in his pockets with an air of diffident authority that interested me, and what was interesting was that the diffidence seemed not to come, as might be expected, from a failure of confidence but from its sudden swelling. Here, I thought, was someone who knew his own strength, someone ready to swim against the Dublin tide of drink and palaver. I was ready for that myself.

"Another time," I said.

"Yes," he said, "certainly another time."

Ten Oona talked a lot about the farm—how she loved and neglected it and felt guilty for spending so little time there. At first she was always saying, "You must come down to Drumfoyle, Ann." Then at a point that appeared to have nothing to do with anything I did or said, this invitation took on the inflection and the language of her worries about the place, and she started saying, "We've dragged you down to Drumfoyle with us, haven't we?" The next thing I knew, it was, "You're not interested in going to the farm, sure you're not." I really wasn't, having no particular love for the country—that is until my first visit to Drumfoyle. It came about one Saturday morning when I was walking along Baggott Street with my market basket loaded. Someone in a passing car began to honk the horn, and I recognized the Morris Minor pulling over to the curb, hands waving from the windows. "We're going down to the farm for the afternoon," Oona called. "Will you come?"

Saturday was a half day on the south side of Dublin. Everything there closed, and you were left to your own devices, or to O'Connell Street with its cheap hamburger restaurants and huge cinemas that mostly showed musicals or westerns. I said, "Let me get rid of my groceries."

Oona and the girls had seemed to me to be on unique terms, but that afternoon I discovered their resemblance to most families. Crammed into the car together the girls picked on each other, Daisy insisting that the week before Annabel had borrowed her blue cardigan without permission, and Annabel who sat up front with Oona repeatedly screaming, "No, I didn't!" Finally Annabel burst into tears and cried, "Mother, make her stop!"

In the back seat Madeleine leaned over to me every so often to practise her trick of chinning on people's shoulders. Daisy would say, "Stop that, Miss Ross," but she laughed after she said it, which infuriated Annabel.

"Anything Madeleine does is funny but with me you're always giving out!"

Oona handled the car with a mixture of haste and reluctance as if she were of two minds about whether we ever got where she was taking us, though once we were deep into the country, she clearly regretted being there. It was mile after beautiful mile of fields interrupted every so often by a village consisting of one long curved street, or a crossroads presided over by that powerful trinity—the grocery shop that was also the pub and the post office. Thirty miles of this brought us to a gate in front of a dirt avenue that divided pastureland where sheep were grazing. Annabel got out and undid the latch, holding the gate open while we passed through; then she got back in the car. At a second gate she said, "I'll walk the rest of the way."

When Oona had said farm, a cluster of buildings and outbuildings always went through my mind, but a solitary house now came into view, a compact place with beautifully kept grounds and a proper suburban gravel drive. "I'd give anything if I didn't have the key," Oona said as she stopped the car and began digging in her handbag. She found her keys and let us in. As I stepped across the threshold I knew I'd never seen anything like that house and probably never would again. It was small but on a grand scale, and everything had been arranged with a thorough understanding of both delight and comfort. Remembering it now, I see the pleasing play of light and shadow which looked, and in a way was, built in—that house was cleverly windowed. I couldn't imagine someone who owned it living anyplace else and I said this to Oona. "Wait," she said and threw open the drawing-room door. "Look!" The rear windows framed fields where there were sheep and cattle, on the far left a small woods, and straight ahead in the near distance the ruined spread of a monastery. Bucolic, I thought, as with a pleasant shock I suddenly knew the meaning of the word. Oona went and opened a door at the back of the room; I followed her outside, and we crossed the lawn which was separated from acres of meadow by a barbed-wire fence; we climbed the stile at one end, and Oona began to talk. "James always said he wished he'd built an outside staircase to his room. He was such a solitary man to be married to someone like me though he loved being a husband. He used to say, 'Why didn't you make me one sooner?'" The truth was he never wanted to get married, and we almost didn't. We were engaged and the date set, when he suddenly disappeared. He'd had to go to Galway on business and while he was there he decided not to see me again."

"How did you get back together?" I asked.

"One day we ran into each other in Findlater's on D'Olier Street. We were married within the month, and I was pregnant the month after. I had a bunch of daisies that day in Findlater's, so James said that was the baby's name."

"Why did he leave in the first place?" I asked.

"He was never very strong physically and he thought he wasn't able for all the work of a marriage. Delicate is an odd word for a man so big and handsome but delicate is nearly the word for him. Sometimes when I can bear it I wonder whether he might have lived longer if I hadn't been so determined. You see what the house is like, and I had to have it—the Georgian silver and the hunt tables and the Old Waterford and the rest." We reached the Abbey, and Oona led me along a roofless cloister, up some broken stairs to a room that had crumbled away to a porch. "Be careful," she warned as I put my elbows on the wall, "you never know when it'll give way." It was a gray but not a dull day, the sky companionably low, as if the masses of cloud had drawn in to listen to Oona. "At first my father didn't like James. He used to say, 'That fellow's no good at all.' When we were married James made up for it, and no one could match him. My father loved him then—I suppose because we were so happy."

I said, "You must have gone mad when he died."

She nodded. "I took the girls to France, and we stayed with friends there, but it wasn't a good idea, so we came back to Ireland, here to Drumfoyle, but that wasn't right either."

"So you went to Stella Philbin's?"

"Then I got word they wanted to make the film of *Three Brothers*. With that money I did up the mews." A figure appeared on the lawn at the back of the house; it was Annabel, who began waving and jumping up and down. "They'll want to be getting back to Dublin," Oona said.

"How can you bear to leave?" I said.

"How can we bear to come?" She led me down through the Abbey, and we started back across the fields. It was a couple of weeks since I'd seen her; in that time Michael had turned up, and I told her about this. "Well so," she said, "and what do you think of him?"

I said, "I'm not sure."

"You might go slowly," said Oona.

That was good advice, but I didn't follow it when Michael rang that Sunday. I'd just got back from Mass. "So you go to Mass on Sunday," he said.

I said, "Yes, don't you?"

"Occasionally."

"I thought it was the thing to do here."

"And is that why you go?"

"No," I said, "I like Sunday Mass."

"What were you having for your lunch?" I told him spaghetti, and he said, "There should be enough for two then."

"Is that a hint?"

"I'll be there in twenty minutes." He hung up, and I began slicing onion and pepper and garlic. I also sliced into my left thumb, had only the smallest size band-aid to cover it with, and was still bleeding when he arrived. "Have you Vaseline?" he asked. I got it, and he sucked the surface blood from the cut and then smeared some of the grease on it. No subsequent touch matches the privileged quality of the first, nothing that follows is more dramatic.

"Vaseline probably isn't antiseptic," I said mildly.

"Probably not but it's better than having you bleed into our food."

"The sauce is tomato," I said. "You wouldn't have noticed."

He'd brought a bottle of wine and as he opened it he said, "That's an interesting stove."

"It's a joke," I said.

"The Finns had a fetish for utensils. There was no such thing with them as a cooker or a dish or a chair serving the purpose. Design was everything. They made a religion of their home life."

"The Irish make a home life of their religion." I said it without thinking and found myself in an argument that my heart wasn't really with and that went on all through lunch.

"Take away religion, and what have you left?" Michael said. "Obsession with appearances." He got up from the table and began pacing the box room.

"If you're such a believer," I said, "why don't you go to Mass on Sunday?"

"That's not the point."

"Maybe not the whole point."

"Do you really love God?" he asked me.

My finger was throbbing painfully. That plus cooking the meal, drinking the wine, and arguing through it all had lowered my resistance, used up my reserves. "I suppose so," I said.

"You're a faithful churchgoer and yet you only suppose!"

"Isn't that what faith is?"

"That's more like it." He smiled and sat down again, taking my hand, tracing the lines with one finger. "Don't let yourself be thrown off the track."

How clear his eyes are, I thought—light clear gray, without shadows and with a hard brightness. "You were only teasing," I said, and he laughed.

"Of course!" We were leaning across the table, looking at each other intently, when he suddenly stood up, saying, "I've brought some journalism I've done that might interest you." I was a little put off by this, but he got the envelope from his coat pocket and gave it to me. "I'll go now," he said.

"You don't have to."

"It's better for the moment."

This was consideration of a high order, and I appreciated it but I was also a little disappointed. When he left, I sat down with the clippings and learned that he'd been all around the world. The articles amounted to a series of comparisons with Ireland, and no place held up: Russian life was regimented and Spain's morally stylized; Japan was compulsive, France was a cliché, England was predictably ineffectual. Reading through all this I grew anxious on Michael Flynn's behalf, for even I knew that Irish nationalism must have an element of mockery. Committing himself in print to pure love of country was foolhardy if not foolish, and I began to think I should try and get this across to him.

Eleven Oona's request that I drop in on her mother was offhandedly put, but I'd rather be guilty of scrupulous attention to such things than of dismissing them and one afternoon I went over to the block of flats. After I'd rung Mrs. Kehoe's doorbell I heard fumbling noises inside, as if she were dropping and shoving things in the struggle to get up and walk, and this went on for a minute or two before the cracked voice called, "Who's there?"

"Oona's friend, Ann Clarke," I said.

The door opened. At first she didn't recognize me; then all the wrinkles in her little face tightened, and her old eyes lit up in a hectic look of pleasure. "Our friend from New York! Come in!" she cried. "Come in, come in, come in! You're just in time for a cup of tea."

I offered to make it, but she sent me into the parlor, where I immediately began wondering how soon I could leave. It was going to be hard—I realized that even before Mrs. Kehoe hobbled in with the tea tray and started talking.

"Well so, Ann," she said, "—Ann, is it? You're from America. And have you ever been to Philadelphia?" I told her I had cousins who lived there but I might as well have said I'd never heard of the place. "Philadelphia's a grand historical city," she said, "home of the Declaration of Independence and the Liberty Bell. My sister went out there when she was seventeen, and twice I visited her. That was how I met Oona's father—we were on shipboard together, and nothing would do but that I marry him, though it took me a year and a half to come round. I had no great desire to marry the way some do. I had my family, the Connors of Sligo, six boys and three girls we were, the envy of the county."

My own mother has the same tale of the wonderful family that no one else ever measures up to, and this compounded my impatience with Mrs. Kehoe. To calm down I let myself think about Michael: in my mind I walked around and around the Green with him, never once mentioning the rain; then I brought him to the box room where I remade the spaghetti dinner, and as we drank our wine and smiled at each other, I clarified my position. "Yes, I believe in God, except for the times when I'm very happy and don't feel that's necessary or when I'm not happy and feel it to be of no use. Though basically I accept that explanation or description for the attraction and the antagonism that exist among people, the suffering and the bliss we're capable of causing one another. Fall, redemption, communion of saints, resurrection—all lives can be diagramed along some comparable curve. When I'd finished putting this case I had him invite me to meet the aunt he'd once lived with, and we put on our coats and went off to her house, and she took to me immediately. This reconstruction of events made a quarter of an hour with Mrs. Kehoe pass pleasantly enough, and I was almost sorry when the doorbell rang. She started to struggle to her feet, but I said, "I'll get it," and went to the door. Annabel had come by.

"I expected you earlier," said Mrs. Kehoe.

"I had hockey," Annabel said. "I'm only just through. What do you want from the shops?"

"Eggs," Mrs. Kehoe said emphatically.

Annabel was young enough to deal with her grand-mother on more or less equal terms and she went and looked in the refrigerator. "You've a half dozen eggs! That'll get you through tonight, surely, and tomorrow one of us will be by again."

"You'll forget, or something will come up, and I'll be left." The old woman quickly worked herself to the verge of tears. "I'm always the last to be considered. No one cares if I'm alive or dead!"

Annabel put her arms around her grandmother and said, "I'll go get your eggs. Is there anything else?" While Mrs. Kehoe came up with a list of groceries, I put on my coat. Annabel suggested that I come to the shop with her, and since I needed bread I went along. I liked Annabel. She was a graceful girl and full of adolescent discontent that made my life seem enviable to me. "You've such beautiful things," she said, as I tied a scarf around my head. "And so many."

"Not compared to most Americans," I said.

"But compared to all the Irish," said Annabel. "Everyone's so poor here. I'd love to be rich and go where I pleased."

"You don't have to be rich for that. You just have to be old enough to work and save some money," I said. "That's what I did."

"If I had money I'd go to Italy or France. I don't know why you came to Ireland."

"I'm glad I did."

My quarter hour of daydreaming gave this remark shades of meaning that Annabel shrewdly picked up. "Mother tells us Michael Flynn rang you. Do you like him?"

I said, "Yes, though I'm not sure why."

Annabel said, as if it were understood, "But he's so handsome!"

Michael was tall and thin. He had a cleft chin, a short nose, a full mouth, wavy hair cut short. His one suit was of the greenish worsted common in Dublin, and he had the patched trousers of an identical suit which he wore with a black turtleneck pullover, or a long-sleeved, black wool polo shirt. His looks and his shabby flair appealed to me, but I didn't understand that they amounted to specifically "good looks" till Annabel Ross said so, introducing a new factor that made my feelings less stable; when he next came by the library, I was keyed up. "Will you come out with me?" he said. This time I didn't ask where, but he told me, as if there should be no misunderstanding. "To Churchtown."

"To the little poem?" I said, and he nodded.

A crowd was waiting at the bus stop outside the Shelbourne, but we managed to get on board the first number fifty-one that came along. From time to time Michael made some comment over the heads of the people standing between us. "My aunt's house is up there," he said at one point, indicating a side street. "The aunt I lived with." I ducked my head and looked out, pleased to have even a passing connection with someone in that perfectly average segment of Dublin life.

The road began to climb, and the bus slowed, wheezing at each new grade, as the view from the window went, in the course of seven or eight minutes, from suburban to pastoral. I was wondering what I'd let myself in for, when Michael said, "The next stop is ours."

"You didn't tell me it was the country," I said, as we dropped onto a dirt footpath.

He said, "It's not. That's the beauty of Dublin. You can leave it completely behind without really leaving it." At the top of the short road crossing the main road there was a small church with a graveyard full of elaborate headstones—Celtic crosses, Madonnas, an angel with majestic wingspread. Across from this was Michael's cottage. "It belongs to the estate down the road," he said as he let me in. I could see he was proud of the place, and it did have a kind of dash, the makeshift but elaborately comfortable style that characterizes the arrangements of men living alone. From the kitchen we turned left to the spare room which was full of old newspapers, cartons of discarded books, cartons of plain junk. On the other side of the kitchen was the room that served as bedroom, living room, dining room, and office. "The view's marvelous," he said, but it was pitch dark now, and I could see only the various shades of night. "The mountains are straight ahead," he told me and drew the curtains. There were pictures on the walls—Van Gogh and Picasso prints, and an oil painting of an old man. "That's my grandfather," he said, and we stood there in a kind of homage.

I said, "How kind he looks."

"He was full of virtue the way some men are full of spite. It touched everything he said and did."

I said, "You were probably lucky to have lived with him," but Michael disagreed.

"No, that was wrong no matter what." In the kitchen he lifted a trap door in the wall and exposed a fireplace; he lit a fire and got a bottle of brandy from the cupboard, saying, "This will warm you."

"*Slainte*," I said, as he handed me a glass.

"Did you learn that from your native speakers?"

I said, "I learned nothing from them—nothing of any use."

"That's the nature of the beast."

"Beast is right."

"Tell me about them." He wiped off a greasy skillet and began frying a sausage and tomato supper.

"They were spoiled and inconsiderate," I said, "and inseparable—that was their worst trait."

"The tribal legacy," said Michael. "It's very strong in Ireland."

"Well, it was awful." How different this was, I thought—leisurely, private, personal. "And they were so dogmatic. You couldn't hope to see Ireland the way they did."

"Which was true, surely."

"But obviously."

"Finish that up."

He refilled the glasses with wine, and we brought our plates into the all-purpose room where we ate by candlelight at a big round table. I had the sense of following a program arranged on my exclusive behalf and in every detail by someone who had studied how best to manage such things, and I liked this. Organization as a component of pleasure is too often overlooked, though Michael was so systematic that it struck me funny. When we'd eaten, and he sat forward and said, "Shall we go to bed?" I laughed and began to clear the table. "I'm serious," he said.

"I know!"

"Would you rather I were frenzied?" He picked me up and staggered over to the bed with me. "I suppose that's better."

"Much better."

"And how is this?" He slid a hand under my sweater and spanned my back from one shoulderblade to the other.

"Better still."

"How narrow you are."

"Minds are narrow," I protested.

"Waistlines, too." He encircled mine.

"Or lives."

"Escapes."

"It still doesn't sound attractive."

"But it is. See how attracted I am."

Faces feel so much harder than they look—the bone inside the smile and the melting glance; by comparison the body is cushiony and accommodating. "You dazzle me," I said. For the quality in his assurance that puzzled me at first had become crystal clear—eroticism was his natural element.

He could afford to hold back in general, knowing how brilliantly he'd come across in this particular atmosphere. I kept wondering how the plan to live a celibate life had taken such a turn, and in the course of the evening he shed some light on that subject.

"Did you ever hear of *Opus Dei?*" he asked. I pretended I hadn't, thinking an explanation that was also a definition would be less defensive and thus truer. He said, "Members live and work just as anybody else does but they say special prayers and they don't marry."

"Oh." I laid my head on his chest.

"After I left home I was at loose ends, and they seemed to offer some stability, so I joined for two years."

"Then what happened?"

"One summer they sent me to France, to Dijon. The family I stayed with had a daughter who constantly came to my room, asking me things or bringing my linen, always some pretext or other to hang on the desk or brush up against me."

"And that was that?"

He rolled over and said, "That was this."

As I put my arms around him I thought of Tomás, wondering what I'd ever seen in him, wishing I'd been less ready to come up with anything at all.

Twelve The vision of Ireland I'd got from Tomás and his friends boiled down to the familiar "land of saints and scholars"—and singers; scholars and singers anyway. Michael Flynn offered a version of the equally romantic "noble peasantry," though it took me a while to recognize the similarity between the two attitudes. Subconsciously I felt that two misses in a row would be unlikely and certainly unfair, that a stroke of bad luck such as I'd met in Tomás must be followed by compensation, as if luck were a product that the manufacturer had an obligation to uphold—and this disposed me to give Michael a hearing. Furthermore, his updating of old ideas made them provocative at first. "They talk of the intellectual French Catholic," I remember his saying. "Why, Irish faith is far more modern."

"Far more?" I said.

"You have only to look at the faces in any church here to see how subtly people think and feel about these things."

I said, "I was told mine is a Galway face."

"By the native speakers?"

I enjoyed being able to pass along the information I'd soaked up during those long nights at the pubs and I kept trying to pass along the skepticism that had come with it. "But then they said Galway was spoiled. And just think—to me Dublin is unspoiled."

"Tell me more."

"They were heartless." I backed up this claim with the story about Liam's wife leaving the phone off the hook, but Michael insisted I'd misinterpreted the gesture.

"She was probably used to that kind of thing. Irish women make excellent wives."

"Out of necessity."

"They're realistic."

"They haven't much choice."

"You don't understand."

More often than not our discussions ended on that note. They were also repetitive. Michael had only a few themes, or rather one theme—the greatness of Ireland, which could be made to fit any particular subject: the Church, the government, the educational system, the pub life, the women's looks, the quality of Irish goods. In the second place my facts of Irish life were not inexhaustible. I sometimes regretted the lost contact with their source, and this in turn put me in a receptive mood one day in late February when I ran into Jim

Larkin on Grafton Street. I'd stopped to examine the books on display in the Eblana window, and the reflection of someone standing behind me caught my attention; I felt I knew who it was even before I turned and looked into those alert and humble eyes.

"I thought it was you," he said, "but I wasn't certain."

"That makes two of us."

Jim Larkin didn't really understand that kind of talk; his own feelings were too strong to be taken lightly, and his speech showed such a primitive respect for words that he sounded stilted. "Have you not been happy?" he asked. I had to tell him I was fooling, and though he didn't quite get the joke he laughed and said, "I'd like to invite you for a cup of coffee. Or would you prefer a glass of beer?"

I said coffee was fine and suggested we go to Bewley's, but he was afraid it might be crowded there. "Let's try," I said.

Bewley's had plenty of empty tables, but when we were seated, he was filled with fresh doubts. "A place that's empty gives you a queer feeling, doesn't it?" I told him not to worry so much. "It's hard not to," he said, "with someone like you."

I picked up the menu and said, "I think I'll have a bun."

A waitress came over, and he gave the order. When she left, there was a really appalling silence; finally I said, "Bewley's is practically my second home."

"Have you got to know Dublin?" he asked.

"Parts of it," I said, and he asked which parts. I could see he was calculating his chances and to keep him off the track as well as relieve his mind I dredged up Tomás—for I could be quite cold about Tomás.

"Were you ever in love with the fellow?" he asked.

I said, "Not really. It was just that he seemed so Irish."

"You should know Ireland better since you like it so well." And he suggested, "I could show you a bit of the country—this corner of it anyhow."

My first reaction was not to get involved; then it occurred to me that I might be of use to Jim Larkin. Knowing someone like me could boost his confidence—not that I was so marvelous but at least I didn't lick my fingers after I finished a bun, the way he did, or spoon up tea when it was too hot to drink. And wasn't it kinder to let him grow tired of me instead of making myself inaccessible and thus more desirable? In return, of course, he'd act as ballast. I didn't like the idea of deliberately playing him off against Michael, but you can get around that by restricting things to museums and the like, by not getting dressed up, and by paying your own way. When the waitress in Bewley's brought the check, I insisted on chipping in, and Jim eventually let me. Out on Grafton Street he said, "If you've not been to Dun Laoghaire we might go there Saturday afternoon, that is if you've nothing else to do. Or would you prefer to stay in Dublin?"

"Dun Laoghaire sounds interesting." The gaunt profile of Proinsias had crossed my mind.

"Shall I call for you?" he asked, but I suggested we meet someplace. "How about the G.P.O.?" he said. "Then if the weather's bad, you can wait inside."

By the time these arrangements were completed, I'd begun having second thoughts. It's dangerous to tamper with someone's affections, and I walked home contemplating the possible repercussions. Jim Larkin was obviously someone who'd get attached to you no matter what. And he was so gawky. I didn't like the idea of being seen with him around town—and town it was, that small city. In my preoccupation I forgot I'd intended to stop at Findlater's, and I was at Pembroke Street before it occurred to me that I was completely out of butter. I turned in at the Monument Creamery and saw Tricia Driscoll sliding patterns into the sawdust on the floor. Beatrice spotted me then, and they came over, and she said, "Isn't it nice to see Ann, Trish?"

"Who?" said Tricia and she began sucking her thumb.

"Quite right, she's a stranger—to some of us anyway." Beatrice gave me a look. "Neil and I ran into Michael Flynn the other night."

My heart did something that gave the effect of shifting gears. I asked, "Where?"

"He showed up at a dinner party we went to. Neil got into a fight with him, and they kept at it all through the meal. Flynn was full of talk about the quote New Ireland unquote. He accused Neil of being *passé*, and Neil called him a cultural adventurer. Do you know him well?"

"I met him at Oona's." Except for that evening, the times I'd spent with Michael were sequestered, which had seemed ideal after Tomás, but now I had to wonder. "Who else was there?" I asked Beatrice.

"Just some stuffy Anglo-Irish. Neil said, at least Flynn livened things up. But watch out for the fellow—he's a bit of a divil."

Tricia said, "The divil has a big long tail."

Beatrice made a face and said, "We got that from Mrs. MacManus, the babysitter."

"And there are two little things that stick up off his head," said Tricia.

"You wouldn't be interested in a little babysitting on the side, would you?" asked Beatrice. "Sometimes Mrs. Mac is pretty heavily booked." I wasn't enthusiastic about the idea. I didn't take to Tricia and I didn't trust myself with her—she wasn't as happy as she thought she was, and I felt myself always in danger of revealing this to her, but when Beatrice said, "I'll call you one of these days," I said that'd be fine.

The company of someone you love requires of you what you long to give; the only question is how much. Other sorts of company demand constant effort of one sort or another— politeness or at least self-control, the discouragement of false hopes, the defense of your own feelings, plus the simple effort to have a little fun in circumstances not conducive to that. On Saturday afternoon I reached the Post Office in a state of reluctance that made Jim Larkin's air of anticipation all the harder to face. He was dressed up: pinstriped suit with a stiff white shirt and a striped tie; as he nervously unbuttoned his jacket, I saw a gold watch chain slung across his waistcoat. I had on my yellow tweed skirt and a gray cardigan buttoned up the back, I hadn't washed my hair and I'd skipped makeup, but when he said, "You're looking marvelous!" it hit me that apparent lack of artifice had its own powerful attraction. "There's our bus," he said and grabbed my hand; then with great delicacy he dropped it, and we set off, making the bus just in time. "Will we sit on the top deck or the bottom?" he asked, and I led the way to the top, where he immediately began to spoil the view, distorting it with his overprecise descriptions. "O'Connell Street is where the working class amuse themselves."

"What an old-fashioned word," I said, " 'working class.' " Nothing about him said either snob or Communist, but he described Merrion Square in the same sort of language.

"This is the *bourgeois* part of the city." It was also my part, and though I knew it was silly to take offense, I understood why Tom Wynne had called him a boor. Then he dismissed Ballsbridge as *"Nouveau riche,"* and I had to reconsider, for that was the perfect description.

"All that red brick respectability," I said, when we'd left it behind.

"Look," he cried, "there's the sea!"

It was off to the left—a flat green dish of water, Dublin Bay. "Where are we?" I asked.

"Booterstown," he said. I was reminded of Cork—the butchers', the draper's, the betting parlors. This scene quickly gave way to another like it, Monkstown; then Monkstown gave way to Blackrock which had a more prosperous look and was the next town to Dun Laoghaire.

The afternoon was raw. There was no rain, but a cold wind off the water made me turn up my coat collar as we began walking. "Maybe we should just have our tea," said Jim.

"Stop worrying." If I were to be useful to him I also had to be tough.

"It's hard not to worry with someone like you," he said.

"And don't be so formal."

He objected to that. "Manners are all there is between us and chaos."

"Not feeling?" I suggested.

"Feeling's the eye of the chaos."

"Only when it gets out of hand."

"One way or another it always does."

The horizon is a sobering spectacle, a reminder of the limits there are to understanding and of the tricks the physical world can play. "The trouble with manners is they tend to be misleading," I said, having in mind Michael—something stylized in our intimacy kept us at a distance from each other.

"Manners only mislead if one of the people is in love," said Jim, "and then the trick is to use them to protect yourself."

"How?" I asked.

"If you cling to them you have a chance at least of staying out of the pit of need." He looked sideways at me. "Have you never found yourself there?"

I made a mental detour and said, "I was thinking of my mother." She gave my sister and me plenty of manners and plenty of love, too, but love of a kind that brings with it the obligation to live up to expectations, not only of you but of life itself. I said as much to Jim Larkin who replied with a line from Yeats.

" 'Hearts are not had as a gift, but hearts are earned by those that are not entirely beautiful.' "

"That shouldn't apply to children."

"It's better to learn early," he said. "My mother died when I was eleven. My father raised me and my sisters, and all he knew of human nature was beating it into submission." It was a Dickensian story, and visions of *David Cop-*

perfield made me shiver in sympathy. He said, "You're cold. Will we have our tea now?"

We went to a seaside *café*, though luncheonette would have been a better word for it. I ordered sausage and tomato, and Jim had spaghetti which he tried to eat with his knife and fork. "You have to twist it." I showed him how, and he thanked me.

"What are your sisters like?" I asked. A boy growing up could get by without learning such things, but it struck me that girls would be under a handicap.

"They're beautiful women," he declared. "The youngest is twenty. She lives here in Dublin. She's a bit in love with me."

Like everything else he said this rang absolutely true, but it was all too much—the beatings, the motherlessness, and now a hint of incest. I said, "I suppose sisters are always a little in love with their brothers." He looked offended and still hadn't got over it when I tried to pay half the check.

"It's not the custom in Ireland," he said with the firmness of someone who however outwardly shaky might be privately in formidable command of himself. This impression stayed with me during the ride home, but on my doorstep the meek Jim Larkin asserted, or rather failed to assert, himself. "Might there be a chance of seeing you again?" he asked. "I'd like to take you to dinner at Jammet's."

In my impatience I said, "Why not!"

For all its awkwardness, the afternoon at Dun Laoghaire had charm; if Jim Larkin was clumsy he was also original, gallant, and sincere. His Ireland was James Joyce country, a painfully vivid but familiar place where I felt more at home than in Michael Flynn's "modern Ireland," and this gave me a sense of detachment that I brought to Churchtown the following day.

"Don't you ever clean this sink?" I asked.

"Of course not," said Michael. "Sinks are for cleaning

in, not for being cleaned." He went into the next room and put on a record.

"Mozart?" When he didn't answer, I wiped my hands, spread the towel to dry, and followed him; he'd opened the french windows and gone outside. "It's funny that Ireland has no musical tradition," I said.

"Nonsense!" He gave me his hand; I stepped out over the ledge and leaned against the house, with my arms folded. It was a sheltered spot—a few yards of flattened grass enclosed by hedges on two sides; the third side sloped down to meadowland, and past this were the mountains, like immense timid presences keeping their distance. "Song is at the very heart of Irish culture," said Michael.

"Whack fol the diddle-o," I said, but he didn't laugh. "Well, I meant classical music," I said.

"For the Irish, sound must be speech."

"And instruments are expensive."

He gave me a slap. "That for your expensive."

I hit him back. "And that for your Mozart."

"It isn't Mozart, it's Tchaikowsky—the Suite No. 4 in G." He stretched out on the ground, one elbow bent, a hand supporting his head, one knee raised. Desire took my breath away, and when I spoke next I sounded as if I'd been running.

"That sounds like Mozart to me."

"Subtitled 'Mozartiana,' " he admitted.

There was a dance in a rather discursive style; then the music moved into the measured and stately mood of a minuet. "Sort of a Mozart sampler," I said and sat down alongside him.

"Mozart is pure enjoyment."

"I'll take Brahms."

"I'm Brahms, watch me suffer!" he said, looking tortured.

I said, "I'm the one who's suffering."

"Shall I put you out of your misery?"

"No, that's all right, leave it on."

"Not that misery."

The centerpiece of Tchaikowsky's "Morzartiana" was the hymn *"Ave Verum Corpus"* in its entirety. At the sound of those first rarefied chords I stiffened, but Michael saw nothing inappropriate about making love to a hymn of praise to the body of Christ. "You're confusing morality and aesthetics," he said.

"They are confused—at least linked. For me anyway." I sat up.

"Everybody isn't like you, Ann. You lump people together, but we're all different."

The word sent a chill through me. "Not that different," I said and lay back again, feeling in my mind for the detachment I'd brought with me to Churchtown, wondering if this might be a situation that would consume detachment as fast as it could be produced.

"There now," he said, as the hymn concluded on chords as rapturous as the first few. "That's enough meditation, don't you think?"

"Yes," I said, "that's enough."

Thirteen   I'd told myself I could be useful to Jim Larkin but I had no such excuse for going out with the Driscolls' friend who rang me up in the middle of February. "Desmond DeCourcy here," he said in his rather thin voice, and my heart sank; then it hardened, and I pretended I'd forgotten the name. "We met with Neil and Beatrice at Christmas," he reminded me. "We were going to do the museum sometime."

"Oh," I said, "that's right," and he took this as an acceptance.

"Are you free Sunday?"

I agreed to meet him outside the museum at half past two. When I hung up and told Dinah what I'd let myself in for, she said, "Cheer up. You'll probably be able to get away after an hour."

But an hour turned out to be no way near enough time to spend at the National Museum, though it was a modest collection. "No miles of spoils from the tombs of kings?" I asked Desmond DeCourcy.

"You must remember, we're an island," he said. "You must also remember that the Romans never got here."

A lot of others did—Celts, Vikings, Anglo-Saxons, and then the English, wave after wave of them. What wasn't destroyed or carried off made a rich collection of daring simplicity and to my mind a certain ambiguity—the Tara brooches were like daggers, the reliquaries were indistinguishable from the relics which they had, in fact, sometimes taken the place of, and both were as gaudy as the crown jewels. "I suppose in a way they *are* our crown jewels," said Desmond DeCourcy. "Holy Ireland, you know." He was a good guide, full of interesting facts that it still gives me enormous pleasure to turn over in my mind: In ancient Ireland warriors sometimes rode into battle naked except for the swords they carried, and the gold and silver ornaments they wore around their arms and necks; Irish craftsmen in the eighteenth century B.C. did work in gold that can be compared to the great period of Irish silver crafts in the eighteenth century A.D.; the Clark find was the greatest discovery of prehistoric gold in Western Europe; the Ardagh chalice, which is seven inches high and takes two hands to lift, was found by workers digging for potatoes.

Without my noticing, the skylight in the museum went from white to gray, and the guards began shepherding people towards the door. Desmond De Courcy asked, "Now shall we have our tea at the Shelbourne?"

I enjoyed parading past the desk with this unmistakable specimen of the Ascendancy, but in the lounge I felt a little foolish sitting down with my elderly companion among the off-season crowd of smart-looking Dubliners. He ordered a full tea which helped; I was buttering my second scone when I noticed him sitting there smiling at me. "You know," he said, "you've a remarkably-shaped head." I put my hands to my hair and took it from behind my ears. "I notice heads," he told me. "Most are flat in back, but yours has a lovely curve. Following you about I was struck by it." This robbed the afternoon of the high tone that was partly responsible for the pleasure I'd got from it, and Desmond DeCourcy recognized this; he began to blush and so did I—I knew I shouldn't have agreed to see him and I felt that I'd pay for the degree of self-interest that made me do so. I also felt that I knew the form my punishment would take: on the way home I'd run into someone I knew, probably Michael. But we made it safely to Fitzwilliam, or so I thought till Tony dropped by the box room. It turned out he'd been following us all the way from Merrion Row.

"Robbing the rocking chair, are you now, Ann?"

"Don't rub it in," I told him.

"How about washing away the taste with a beer at Mooney's?"

"Not tonight, thanks," I said. "It's been a long day."

"Ah well, if you're too busy for your old friends."

"Don't be silly," I said.

"Silly am I? What about the dinner you were going to cook for me?"

"Name the day."

"How about Tuesday week? Mind you," he said, "I'm expecting a proper meal. None of your sausage and chips."

I decided to take Tony seriously, and the day he came to supper, from four o'clock on my room smelled powerfully of wine and garlic. As Dinah was leaving she looked in on me and asked, "What *are* you cooking?"

"*Coq au vin*," I said. "I've never made it before."

"If it doesn't turn out, don't worry—the aroma's as good as a meal."

The *coq au vin* did turn out. "I'm impressed," Tony said. "If I'd known you were this good a cook I'd have been having my dinner here regularly."

"It's beginner's luck," I said, "believe me."

"Don't be modest," he said.

"I'm not." But Tony obviously discredited this. We weren't at all the same type and ordinarily would never have got to know each other. His mind was too literal, his interests too scientific for me, and we really had nothing to talk about, with the result that I had to knock myself out, though things got easier as the evening wore on, for he'd brought a bottle of wine. We were sitting over the last of it when I told him about Barbara's visit which was then three weeks away. "We're supposed to drive around the country, but so far I haven't done a thing except rent the car."

He pushed his plate to the side and with one finger plotted a route for me. "Start here in Dublin and drive as fast as you can across the midlands to Galway. When you get there, go straight to Connemara."

"Wait a second, let me write this down." I went and got pencil and paper, and Tony continued.

"Take the coast route through Connemara—it's marked on all the maps: Maam Cross, through the Twelve Bens, and so on. Then back you go to Galway City. You might cross over to Aran while you're there."

"Someone told me to skip it," I said.

"Pay no attention. Aran's a beautiful wild place, and be sure to go through Clare and take in the Burren—marvelous limestone fields. The flowers will just be starting to push through the cracks when you're there. Afterwards, shoot on down to Kerry and out to Dingle. Dingle's another wild place."

I said, "Tell me someplace civilized to go."

"Nothing's civilized in Ireland," Tony said. "You're here

long enough to know that—our civilization's in ruins. Does your sister fancy antiquity?"

I said, "I suppose so." Barbara studied painting in school and she had real talent though not the desire that's necessary if someone's to make a go of it in that direction. She didn't want to teach drawing, and after college she got a job with an advertising agency, but by the time she realized what a dead end that was, it was too late to start painting seriously, and she still didn't want to teach, so she went and got a degree in French. Now she works as a translator, but it's an exacting job, and she's never really been content with it.

Tony said, "Go to Clonmacnoise, anyway. The ruins there are worth seeing."

"Was that a knock at the door?" Thinking Theresa might have stopped by with a message, I called, "Come in!"

A man and a woman with their heads together, an empty wine bottle between them—the sight seems to speak for itself, though clearly Mrs. Philbin thought she'd got the message before she even opened the box-room door. "So sorry to interrupt," she said with a self-deprecating and forgiving smile.

"We were just having dinner," I said and I added, "It's the first time I've used the oven."

She raised her eyebrows, no doubt remembering my insistence on having one. "I won't keep you," she said. "I only wanted to ask if you'd care to go to the ballet—a friend who couldn't use her tickets gave me the pair. But I see you're not free." In fact I was. After supper Tony would be off to the library, and I had nothing else to do; but Mrs. Philbin's invitation wasn't negotiable—not that I had any desire to negotiate an evening in her company. "Perhaps another time," she said and slipped back out of the room, closing the door softly behind her.

Tony pushed his chair away from the table. "Perishing ballet!"

I said, "I suppose it was nice of her to invite me."

"You should have taken her up on her invitation. Then

you'd have seen whether there were any flipping ballet tickets!" He looked at me and sighed, and I saw what a lonely and troubled fellow he was—ambitious, fretful about his ambitions, and in general highly susceptible. It was silly of me to have ignored appearances, for things are always to some degree what they seem to be.

Beatrice called me that week. "Remember your promise?" she said, and my mind went blank. "That you'd sit with Trish. Neil and I are going to a party tonight, and Mrs. MacManus is down with the flu."

When I was growing up, babysitting had yet to become big business, and the only child I ever minded was my mother's youngest brother's oldest son. He was a funny little boy and a bold one, always trying to escape notice and put something over on you, but Tricia Driscoll did everything she could to hold my attention that night. Poor thing—she had every right to expect something special, considering the buildup her mother gave me when I arrived. "You remember Ann Clarke, don't you, Trish? She's your great friend and tonight she's going to mind you. Won't that be fun?"

"But where's Mrs. Mac?" Tricia asked.

Beatrice said, "She's sick." Tricia stuck out her lower lip. "Daddy and I are going to leave now. Be a good girl and go to bed when you're supposed to." Tricia began to cry. "Don't worry," Beatrice said to me, "that's just for effect."

As soon as Neil and Beatrice left, the tears did stop, and Tricia led me back into the living room where two entire walls were lined with books. "What should we do?" she asked.

"What do you usually like to do?" I moved in to read the titles—everything from the latest Simenon to precious rarities from the Yeatses' *Cuala* Press.

"I like to do Irish dances, and I like to jump rope, and I like to have a doll party. And best of all I like to play Simon Says."

Maybe she'd go to bed early, I thought. "What shall we do first?"

"But what would *you* like to do?" She was used to being told how to play which irritated me and led me to take the easy way.

"Let me see your Irish dancing." I don't know what I expected—surely not flawless or even competent execution of those quick steps—but when Tricia started spinning in heavy circles I stupidly disapproved. "Here," I said, "watch me." I showed her the basic jig I'd learned back in parochial school, but Tricia's problem was a lack of rhythm. After ten minutes of her Irish dancing, I said, "I guess that's enough."

"What should we do now?"

I looked at the books and told myself that the sooner she got tired, the sooner she'd go to bed. "How about a game of Simon Says?"

"I'll be Simon."

Even for a child she was too self-centered, though I thought I understood why. Lovable and all as Neil was, he really wasn't much of a father—in fact he seemed in his quiet way to claim the spotlight that in other families belongs to the children. Having to learn to capitalize on whatever came her way had made Tricia subject to fits of boisterousness, and she was a theatrical Simon. I played along, holding back and pretending she was too quick for me, until I realized she was getting worked up, not tired out. "I think it's time for a story," I said. She was the one who began to tell it when we were seated on the sofa. So much the better for the sitter, I thought and leaned back.

"Once upon a time there was a beautiful princess from Michigan."

"Michigan? I didn't know they had princesses there."

"*Michigan!* Her name was Beatricia, and she had everything she wanted, dresses and rings and a fur coat and a car and everything. Then one day a big rough man came along, and his name was Bog-Man because he came from the bogs."

"Are there bogs in Michigan?"

"I mean the Irish bogs!"

Poor Tricia—on the sidelines of her own life, obliged to

reinvent the other characters in order to come to grips with them. But I wasn't so sorry for her that I didn't welcome half past eight when it finally arrived, though I was ashamed of being selfish and as I tucked the covers around her I gave her a kiss.

"I like you, Ann Clarke," she said. "Will you sit with me again?"

Fourteen The steady winter rain had given way to showers, and during the spells of strong, damp sunlight you practically had to push your way through the crowd on Grafton Street. The Green came into its own: everyone walking to or from town cut through there; the deckchairs were unloaded from the bandstand and set up along the main paths; children gathered at the pond to feed the ducks or to fish for sticklebacks which they caught with stiff gauze nets and stored in jam jars. This was the Dublin spring, a subdued affair, but ecstatic in its effect on me. I felt myself always on the verge of some happy revelation, some high point, and in this state I called Michael at nine o'clock on a Thursday night and told him I was coming out to Churchtown.

He said, "I'll be up early tomorrow. I'm off to Limerick to give a talk on Church art."

"Then I won't come," I said.

"No, do. It's a good idea. We'll have a nice night."

When I got there twenty minutes later, the house looked deserted, but the front door was open; I walked in and called to him, and he called back—from the bedroom, I thought, but he was in the bathroom in the tub. I leaned over and splashed him, kissed him. "Get in with me," he said.

"I had a bath yesterday."

"Don't Americans bathe daily?"

"I don't," I said. "Not here. It's too cold." I handed him a towel, and he got up and dried himself, followed me to the bedroom and began assembling things—a candle stuck to a dish, a box of matches, a glass of water, an alarm clock, a book. When he'd positioned them on the night table he lay down and watched me undress.

"How white your underwear is," he said.

"American nylon," I said. "It's the best."

"It should be. You invented the stuff." He made room for me beside him.

"And now what would the rest of the world do without nylon?"

"Return to Irish linen. We'll have a renaissance. We'll become an industrial giant with factories everywhere."

"No more countryside?"

"And no more tourists—or a better class. The roads will be full of Jaguars and Bentleys. Our women will all wear mink and diamonds, and they'll smell wonderful. There'll be Frigidaires and clothes washers galore."

"That comes from the Irish," I said, "*go-leór*—one of the few words I learned."

"We'll be the new playground of the world! There'll be casinos at Killarney, yachts in Galway Bay!"

"Stop." It bothered me that he was so easily carried away, for even happy love has a trace of sadness or at least sobriety, always the recognition on some level that things are perpetually, if only in small ways, ending. Though the trouble with that night was that it kept on going. Nights of love are known for their languorousness, but love can also be a stimulant, and that was the trouble—I couldn't get to sleep.

"It's a skill," he said. "You must cultivate sleep, Ann." He closed my eyes with his hand and said, "Look at the colors. Keep focusing your attention and you'll drop off."

"I see a sort of picture," a fuzzy image of his face, like a poor silkscreen impression.

He sat up and lit the candle. The bed became an island of low intense light that made the rest of the room look fantastic. He took a drink of water, gave me some, and then reached for the book. "Listen to this," he said. " 'As stolen love is pleasant to a man, so is it also to a woman; the man dissembles badly; she conceals desire better. She will not come floating down to you through the tenuous air, she must be sought, the girl whom your glance approves.' " His voice quickened, and he began bringing out the mocking tone of the dry text. " 'Sooner would birds be silent in spring or grasshoppers in summer, or the hound of Menelaus flee before the hare than a woman persuasively would resist a lover; nay, even she, whom you think cruel, will be kind.' "

I took the book from him and read the title: Ovid, *The Art of Love*. "Tell me a real story," I said, "a true one."

He folded his arms under his head. "When I was fourteen I had to leave school for a year. My father got T.B., and my mother needed me to help in the shop. I was at the head of my class and I kept thinking my father would die and I'd never go back to school. When I did I was out of step, older than the others and smarter."

"That's a horror story," I said, but indignation wasn't called for.

"Irish life is like that," he said, "and anyhow those things always work out. I didn't waste time with the other kids and I got a scholarship to university." He picked up the book again and turned some pages. " 'Let your toga fit, and be spotless; do not let your shoestrap be wrinkled; let your teeth be clear of rust, and your foot not float about, lost in too large a shoe, nor let your stubborn locks be spoiled by bad cutting; let hair and beard be dressed by a skilled hand. Do not let your nails project and let them be free of dirt.' "

"That part ought to be published in *The Irish Times*," I said.

"Are you getting drowsy?"

"Not really."

"I am. It's half past two." He wet his thumb and first

finger and touched them to the flame; the candle went out with a soft hiss. "Let's try and sleep."

I lay quietly till I heard him begin breathing through his mouth, a low soughing sound like the shush of sea against shore on a summer night. People sometimes reveal themselves differently in sleep, but when I turned and looked at him I found the same energetic figure that he was when awake—then for a second I thought he was; he'd raised his right hand as if he were about to lecture me on Irish life, but the next minute he rolled onto his side. He was right about one thing, I thought—sleep *is* a skill. When you were asked whether you'd slept well, it was as if that were a standard of social accomplishment, like being able to dance or to make conversation. Sheep, I thought—people counted sheep. I closed my eyes, bringing to mind the flock at Drumfoyle— dowdy creatures with fat bodies, skinny legs. When I tried to get them to jump a fence in my mind, they became school- boys in blazers and caps, circling and jeering at one of them who was taller than the rest. I opened my eyes again. The hands of the alarm clock had barely moved, but I knew that before I was ready for it the sun would be there, and then the birds. "Try and sleep," he'd said. As if trying were any good—not trying was what did it in the end. One minute you were still hanging on and the next minute you'd let go. One minute you were treading the treacherous waters of the night; a minute later you'd sunk like a stone. One minute you were desperate, a spinning mind and a sore stiff body. The next minute without feeling or knowing, without caring any more, you were gone. . . .

"So you finally dropped off."

There was no sun, but the room was bright; I covered my eyes with one arm. "I didn't hear the alarm."

"I woke early and turned it off."

He came over to the bed. He was wearing his good trou- sers and his black wool polo shirt. I took his hand and examined it. "Your nails project a bit. Otherwise your person pleases," I said, and he smiled.

"Why don't you spend the day here? You'd enjoy having some room, wouldn't you, after that little place of yours?" He went to the closet for his jacket.

"When will you be back from Limerick?"

"It all depends."

I sat up and put the pillow at my back. "My sister's coming over next week, and we're driving to the west."

"I've left some coffee on the stove, and there's bread and bacon. Slam the door after you when you go out." He kissed me goodbye and left.

I lay there till the aura of his recent presence faded; then I got up and poured myself a cup of coffee and made a tour of the house. Objects I'd hardly taken notice of previously, stood out now in his absence, inviting me to make something of them. His records were correct: a little Bach, a lot of Mozart, some Beethoven, some Irish traditional music, plus the complete *Peer Gynt*—probably a side effect of the Scandinavian stay, not the sign of a secret vein of pure romance.

I sat back on my heels to look at the books: *Das Kapital, Thus Spake Zarathustra, The Crock of Gold,* Pascal's *Pensées.* He owned few novels, and those were classics; the several volumes of poetry were mostly translations from the Irish, plus a few Latin originals; and there was the book on Hieronymous Bosch that he'd told me about. I took it from the shelf and turned the pages of color plates till I came to the *Garden of Delights,* that fantastic world of pale, slender, naked creatures whose look of innocence spelled their doom—so much was clear. But what was the significance of the various black men, each holding or wearing an apple? Why were bodies sticking out of a giant mussel shell? Were those flesh-colored spheres supposed to resemble human organs? People trapped by the flesh? But what did the enormous birds and fishes represent? What were those hunting parties after? And the packs of mermaids and mermen? Surely it signified more

than just the assorted nature of pleasure. Were those mountains or dwellings of some kind in the distance? Was the Garden a place of torment or of supreme satisfaction? I put the
book back and went into the bathroom. The medicine cabinet contained a couple of used razor blades, a half molted
shaving brush, and a surprising bottle of hair cream. I opened
it, recognized Michael's smell, and rubbed some cream inside
each wrist; then I washed my face and scrubbed my teeth
with a finger.

Back in the bedroom I wrapped myself in the black turtleneck and went and made some toast and had the rest of
the coffee, but alone in the house I was uncomfortable, dis-
turbed by the clear evidence of habits and tastes contrary to
my own, and after I washed the dishes I decided to leave;
then I had the idea of writing a note. On the desk was a stack
of typing paper under a snow-scene paperweight, but no pen
and only a pencil stub; with a faint, thrilling sense of
transgression I opened the top drawer. I wasn't looking for
trouble, and so the two photographs among the litter of paper
clips came as a shock. In one, a girl was standing against a
fence; in the other, Michael and this girl had their arms around
each other. She was as tall as he was and she had blond hair—
a Finnish girl, left behind in Helsinki or Turku, and no present threat, I told myself, for part Irish was surely a step beyond
Nordic, but this was insufficient comfort in the face of the
truth that now moved from the back to the front of my mind—
there was a step beyond me; in terms of Irish accreditation,
there was someone who could prove me to have been a mere
halfway house. I put the snapshots back, shut the desk
drawer, and left the place as fast as I could.

Fifteen "It's odd nobody ever brought you to /Jammet's before."

"It's too expensive," I said, wishing I were there with someone other than Jim Larkin. How much of his library salary would be wasted on this dinner? Prices notwithstanding, Jammet's lacked frills though it had style, a cozy elegance that made me feel as if I were in someone's living room where tables had been set up to accommodate a fairly large and sedate family party.

"I'd have thought that for you anyone'd hang the cost."

I was trying to pretend he hadn't said this when the bus boy who'd come to fill our water glasses put down the pitcher, crying, "Mr. Larkin, sir! I never expected to see you here!"

"Cummings from Clanbrasil Street, isn't it?" said Jim. He wasn't the least fazed, and I had to admire him for that.

"Are you still at the library, sir?"

"For my sins," said Jim. "You haven't been round in a while."

"I've no time since I took this job." Shaking his head in regret and wonder the boy went off and was followed by a heavyset old waiter who recommended the tomato soup.

"That'll give you a good solid base, anyway," he said. I asked what *poulet sauté Jammet* was. "Ah, that's only breast of chicken in a sort of cream sauce, maybe with a few mushrooms," he said, "and the bit of cheese."

"I'll have that," I told him, and Jim said he'd have the same.

"You'll be safe enough there," said the old man and he gathered up the menus and limped off.

Jim carefully unfolded his napkin, aligned his silverware, and then looked up at me, saying, "I'm surprised you don't know the sort of man who could afford to take you here." I could see I was in for it. "Do you still see that fellow from Cork?" he asked.

"That was finished long ago."

"And is there no one else?"

I didn't know what to say and so I said nothing, but I wasn't to be let off—the evening had a purpose, as evenings generally do. We hadn't got through the tomato soup, when he blurted out, "Is there any chance for me?"

I let myself briefly consider the prospect: a flat or maybe an attached house on the north side of the city. There'd be festive occasions like this one but more frequent evenings at the pub or the pictures. Summer holidays in Kerry, after- noon teas at Bewley's. Wasn't that what I was after? "The librarian's wife," I said to myself but I didn't like the sound of it.

At this point our old waiter intervened with the chicken. Jim took a bite and said, "Would you think there's wine in this cream sauce?" I told him I thought there was, and his eyes lit up. "It's a good dinner, isn't it?" he said. It was and it kept him occupied; so did Cummings, the bus boy, who darted over from time to time, filling our wine glasses, call- ing our attention to a table across the room where pressed duck was being served, describing the possibilities that lay ahead of us in the way of dessert. But both of us ordered vanilla ice cream, to his great disappointment. When it was brought, he volunteered the information, "People here take liqueurs and such after their meal."

"Nothing more for me," I said.

"Just the bill," said Jim. While we were waiting, he said quietly, "There's no chance, is there?"

"I don't think so." He looked as if the preparations he'd made for this answer weren't enough to sustain him. I said, "I'm not good enough for you," but he put it more accu- rately.

"You mean you couldn't love me."

In a way I couldn't even stand him but in another way I looked up to him. His purity of heart was as awesome as it was exasperating.

"Will we still be friends?" he asked desperately.

I felt I was compounding the error in judgment that had made me start seeing him, but I said, "Certainly."

Sixteen Airports are futuristic places, reeking of progress and prosperity, and Dublin Airport is no exception, which makes it an unlikely setting for some of the scenes that take place there—emphasizing the pathos of the *personae* even as it makes them look dated and unseemly, those weeping mothers and grim fathers who must bid goodbye to sons or daughters still obliged in this day and age to go abroad to try and make their way, leaving behind sisters and brothers relegated to lives that will be irremediably rural. As I stood around waiting for my own sister to arrive I felt guilty at having ahead of me nothing more crucial than a holiday. At half past eleven the flight from New York was announced, and I went and positioned myself at the gate. Barbara was the second one through and like the *émigrés* she had tears in her eyes. Unlike most of them she carried nothing but a raincoat and her shoulder bag. "No hand luggage?" I said.

"I checked all three suitcases." Barbara packs for the emergency that will probably come some day and vindicate her, though if I happen to be around for the crisis I'll probably deal with it better, being the more practical. "Ten days is a long time," she said. We went over to the belt to wait for her baggage, and I outlined the arrangements I'd made. "Hey," she said, "you've developed an accent."

"I have?" My spirits lifted. "You'll like Buswell's. It's a typically Irish hotel."

"I still wish I were staying with you."

Even if the box room had been large enough, I'd have been reluctant to share it. The life I'd led there was the most private I'd ever known, and it was vital to me to preserve that. "The flat's really tiny," I told Barbara.

"It's funny to hear you use that word," she said.

"Isn't that your plaid case?" At the customs check an immensely fat man glared at us as if we were a couple of prime suspects and then winked and chalked the cases without so much as snapping a catch. "The bus stop's this way," I said. I understood that I was staking out this foreign city as my territory, but the point was too subtle, and Barbara missed it.

"Let's take a taxi," she said and she found the cabstand herself.

As we drove off, I broached the subject that we must always get out of the way when we see each other after even a brief separation. "How are things at home?"

Barbara lifted her shoulders as if to say, "Now that you mention it," and I groaned. Something in me wants more than anything not to have to worry about my family, not to be continually threatened by their failure to understand or at least manage their lives. Barbara said, "Daddy set the car on fire," and I groaned again. "He dropped cigarette ash in the front seat and then left it in the parking lot. A policeman noticed smoke billowing out, and he broke in and managed to drag the seat onto the ground."

"The carelessness," I said.

"That looks like a palm tree," said Barbara.

I turned to the window. "The other is called a monkey puzzle."

"Isn't it hideous!"

"We pick up the car tomorrow. Today the only thing I've got planned is supper with Oona Ross."

"That sounds nice."

There was no way my sister could have known that nice wasn't the word for Oona, but the trouble is, what Barbara doesn't know takes some toll on the information I acquire for myself, and when we're together I'm inclined to play things down in order to keep my own fund of experience from being devalued. "Don't expect too much of Dublin," I said. "It's a plain sort of place."

But Barbara's hopes are always high. On the other hand she takes disappointment better than I do, and the room at Buswell's with its rickety furniture and the view of an air shaft didn't bother her a bit. "I'll be here such a short time," she said.

"Shall I leave and let you collect yourself?"

"No, stay. I don't want to lose a minute."

We'd have done better to write off that first day, which began deteriorating at Bewley's. Barbara described it—unjustly, I felt—as a cross between Schrafft's and the Automat. I insisted she have sausages, but they gave her indigestion. Afterwards, strolling down Grafton Street and over to the Liffey, I was seized by a kind of *jamais vu* whereby Dublin began to look unfamiliar to me, the life I'd lived there a figment of my imagination. I was quietly distraught, and Barbara was suffering from jet lag by the time we took the bus back across town to Fitzwilliam Square. It was half past three, the hour when schoolchildren were free to see the dentist, and we caught Dinah as she was rushing between the phone and the door. "Can I lend you anything?" she asked. "Dishes or anything?"

"We'll mostly be eating out," said Barbara who has a tendency to speak when I'm spoken to, and another tendency to try and think for me. When I brought her into the box room, she said, "You can't possibly cook on that stove!"

"It's perfectly adequate," I said, remembering my innu-

merable protests to the contrary. I went and lit the fire, and
Barbara began yawning. "Do you mind if I stretch off?" she
said.

"Go ahead. I'll sit here and do some work." That was
how I'd begun to describe the entries in my notebook.

I wouldn't really mind being the younger, I wrote, *if only I
didn't have to keep stepping out of that role and taking over. It's
always having to ignore things and then always having to point
them out that drives me crazy, and that's basically the problem
between Barbara and me.*

I began to worry about bringing my sister to meet Oona
and the girls who noticed and reacted to—usually magnify-
ing—every little thing, but I underestimated Barbara who
after all is pretty, pleasant and intelligent. I also failed to take
into sufficient account the way Oona's interest in people
transcended like or dikslike. When I introduced them, she
said, "We've been longing to meet you, Barbara," and I realized that was true though in a sense that had to do only
superficially with my sister and me—once brought to her
attention, Oona wanted the pieces in a picture to be filled in,
and so did the girls.

Madeleine said, "Are you older or younger than Ann?"

"Two years older," Barbara told her.

"Do you get along?" Madeleine asked, and when Barbara answered that we did, perfectly, Madeleine said, "I don't
believe you. Everybody fights with their sisters."

"How do you like Ireland so far?" Oona asked and then
laughed; but Barbara didn't see anything foolish or obvious
about the question nor about her answer.

"It's beautiful. I can't wait to see all the rest."

"Ah well, we're small but not that small," Oona said.
"You must pick out a couple of bits, otherwise you'll see
nothing."

"Just don't get too close or it'll soon seem quite hideous," said Daisy. "I suppose Ann's told you that." Barbara
gave me a baffled look, as if to say, "I thought you loved it
here!"

Annabel then made her entrance down the spiral staircase. "Why is everybody roaring?" she said. "Ann Clarke's sister must think we're horrid."

But Barbara was impressed by Oona and the girls. "I met the most interesting family," she'd tell people when she got home. I was glad to have given her this but I hate having something important to me reduced to a topic of someone else's conversation and I began to dread the week ahead.

The sun was shining at half past ten as we drove out of Dublin, but after twenty minutes it began to drizzle. The car I'd rented was an American compact that seemed huge on the narrow Irish roads, and Barbara was nervous when it was her turn at the wheel. "Am I all right on that side?" she kept asking, as we rolled through gray villages and fields of yellow flowers, past flocks of sheep and bands of children and solitary workers making insignificant highway repairs with primitive tools. The roll comes to a stop in my mind at a spread of ruins, Clonmacnoise, where we got out and tiptoed around—and still our heels kept sinking in the soggy ground. Out loud Barbara read her guidebook's angry remarks: " 'This, the most famous of Irish monastic cities, was the object of insistent plundering throughout the centuries till 1552 when the settlement was utterly ruined by the English garrison of Athlone who carried off every scrap of glass in the windows.' " She closed the book and said, "A place like this ought to be restored."

I said, "I like it this way." All that remained of the settlement were two round towers, a graveyard, and the shells of eight or nine buildings that I thought were more hospitable for being not only without glass in the windows but without roofs and floors as well. "The past seems more present than if it were all rebuilt," I said. "And more past."

Barbara put up the hood of her raincoat. "It's really coming down," she said, and we went back to the car.

By half past two we were having lunch of greasy lamb chops at the Royal Hotel restaurant in the infamous Athlone.

Barbara said, "Well, now I know one thing about Ireland—grilled means fried."

"There's a hotel in Salthill that's supposed to have a good restaurant. Salthill's a few minutes from Galway." I looked at my watch. 'We should be there in about an hour."

But two separate encounters with skittish flocks of sheep delayed us, and it was after four when we got to Galway. Barbara decided to wash some clothes, while I took a walk around that tiny, fantastically busy place, imagining what it would be like to live there. I thought of Michael and wondered if he were still in Limerick and how far away that was; and I pictured him addressing an audience composed exclusively of plump women with pretty faces like the women in the streets of Galway.

Back at the hotel, Barbara was waiting for me. "Let's have dinner," she said. I pointed out that it was only half past five, but she said, "I'm starving," and so we got dressed and drove to Salthill where, in the face of a stupendous purple sunset over Galway Bay, it seemed crude to be digging into a roast chicken dinner. "Just imagine if we'd grown up here," said Barbara.

I said, "In all probability it would have been Cork."

"Cork, Galway—are they that different?"

"You might as well compare Dallas with Boston." I'm forever trying to make Barbara be more accurate; then as if she'd read my mind, she hit a nail on the head.

"You sound like the guidebook."

A dance was on at the Salthill Ballroom, and as we walked around the town after dinner we were drawn to the music. Men and women in opposing rows of bleachers were sitting watching the few couples who'd ventured out on the floor; then a master of ceremonies announced something called, "The Siege of Ennis."

"A dance named after a battle?" said Barbara.

Everybody climbed down and gathered in circles, hands joined, bodies held rigid as they cut the heavy figures of a rough country dance; when it was over the band swung into a pop song, and a fellow with a red face and huge hands came up and asked me to dance. "I don't want to leave my sister," I said.

"She'll get her own fellow, sure she will." As he said this, another farmer came over to Barbara, and all four of us went out onto the floor. My partner held me as if he thought I might escape, but he wasn't a bad dancer. I suppose he'd had a lot of practice. What other diversion was there in a place like Salthill? "Do you do the rock and roll?" he shouted in my ear.

"Which rock and roll?" I said and hoped the band wouldn't give him a chance to demonstrate.

"Don't all Yanks do the rock and roll?" he shouted.

I said, "I'm not a Yank."

"Not a Yank!" he cried and led me into a spin. Coming out of this I caught sight of Barbara leaving the dance floor alone, and when the music ended, I went over to her.

"I think that fellow just propositioned me!" she said.

"You think?"

"He said, 'Come outside with me. I want to show you my appendix.' " I could only laugh at the ineptitude of it, but Barbara was furious. "Grubby little peasant!" she said.

When the music started up again, my farmer came back, but I told him we were leaving. "Will I see you here next week?" he cried.

"That's a date," I said.

Barbara was still furious when we got back to the hotel, and I suggested we go to the lounge for Irish coffees which I couldn't or at any rate didn't resist calling an American concoction. She said, "I could use a touch of home."

I'd got a map and marked off the route through Connemara that Tony had plotted on my table, and the next day we set off. If you could describe the landscape of feeling, the geography of the heart, it would be those mountains standing in folds against each other, overlapping as moods overlap; the small black lakes spreading like pools of doubt and uncertainty; and over it all the drifting light that characteristically obscures the foreground and strikes a distant hillside, the way hope will point up the future. The drive took about six hours, including lunch of brown bread and ham which we bought at a shop and ate by the side of the road, just past Kylemore. "Visually it's a beautiful country," Barbara said. She'd got out a pad and was sketching Kylemore Abbey which looked like a palace and was smothered in foliage. "But there's something confining, even about Irish space."

"American life can be pretty confining too." I lay back and listened to the silence, as absorbing and as stirring as music.

"The ground is damp," Barbara said. "Why don't you sit on a piece of this newspaper?"

I sat up again. "Barbara," I said, "I'm twenty-six. I know all about catching cold."

She closed the pad and began gathering up the lunch papers. "What about the Aran Islands?" she asked. "Shouldn't we go there while we're nearby?"

"They're supposed to be not worth the trip," I said.

"And you hear so much about them." I knew the subject wasn't closed, and the next morning as soon as I opened my eyes, Barbara said, "How about the Aran Islands?"

I sulked all the way over on the boat, but as we glided into the harbor at Inishmore I forgot that the excursion hadn't been my idea. It was like sailing into some wintry Tahiti—a lush, cold place where life seemed arduous and satisfying. "I could stay here forever," I said, but there was barely time for lunch at the guesthouse and a mad, uphill dash to the prehistoric fort at the top of Dun Aengus. There Barbara breathlessly planted an emotional flag which to this day she waves from time to time: "I'm certainly glad I didn't let you talk me out of the Aran Islands. It's the one place in Ireland I wouldn't have missed."

I was scornful of Barbara's camera but I borrowed it on four occasions and photographed a fuchsia hedge, a blue Kerry mountain with its peak scarved in mist, a white horse grazing in a field of heather, a Palladian manor house seen through a gap in the surrounding wall. Sometimes I look at these pictures now but always with disappointment. They can't compare with the visions of fabulous calm, dishevelment, pleasing austerity, and perfect freshness that invade my thoughts from time to time, destroying my peace of mind with images of the west of Ireland.

Entering Ballyvaughan at dusk we heard music and pulled over to the curb; a minute later half a dozen men in formation, wearing suits and hats and playing shiny band instruments, marched out of an alley and down the main street to the tune of "Deep in the Heart of Texas." On Saturday morning, just outside Kilkee, we passed a wedding party leaving the church, and as I turned around for another look, a gust of wind blew the bride's veil straight up from her red hair—like smoke over fire. On the strand at Ballybunion, we met a man and a boy leading a couple of cows along the packed sand; on the man's head was a handkerchief knotted at the corners to make a cap which he lifted with a smile, saying, "How are you keeping?"

The weather had turned warmer, and I pointed this out to Barbara. "See? We're going south."

She said, "It still feels like November." That she wasn't really taken with Ireland, weather or otherwise, meant I could keep the country intact instead of having to divide it with her, and I was glad of this, but my pleasure in everything had to suffer from being exposed day after day to someone else's distaste. Gradually I began to notice the meagerness of the little towns rather than their charm. I felt cooped up in the car but I managed to get a sore throat. When we reached Killarney, Barbara wanted to see the Lakes, but I said, "Nobody goes to the Lakes of Killarney," and this time I was adamant.

Killarney had a dance hall like the one in Salthill, and as

we walked through the town after dinner we kept passing couples who'd stopped in doorways on their way to the hall and were standing there kissing. "There's something sordid about it," said Barbara.

"They're just unsophisticated," I said. "We're in the heart of the country."

"It'd be different in provincial France," she said.

"Would you rather be getting pinched all the time?"

"That's probably a lot healthier," she said, and I had to concede the truth of this. "I suppose people who are inhibited can't help being furtive," she said.

"The Irish aren't all inhibited." Certainly not Michael Flynn nor Tomás O'Domhnaill. "That's just propaganda."

"These people don't know how to enjoy themselves." Barbara has a sybaritic streak. She likes rich food, expensive shoes and handbags, pure percale sheets, perfumed baths; whereas I'm something of a stoic and I felt it was true to the dire nature of passion that the couples in the doorways should have been driven to take their pleasure where they found it.

I said, "Anyway you can't go by Killarney. This is a tourist town, Barbara."

"So is Antibes."

The next afternoon we were sitting in the Great Southern lounge, eating tomato sandwiches, surrounded by tourists wearing plastic raincoats. I turned to Barbara and said, "Are you dying to see Cork?"

"I suppose not," she said, "not especially. Why?"

"I'd like to ask Oona if she'd let us use the farm. It'd be the most Irish thing we could do, really."

I didn't have to sell Barbara on the idea, but she was doubtful about our chances of getting Drumfoyle. "I can't imagine anyone handing over a place like that."

I rang Oona and put it to her, and she said, "Of course."

Members of your family have one great advantage over other kinds of company—with family there's nothing to explain, no frame of reference to be filled in, no long history of motivation to be laid out and justified. This sometimes makes up for the ancient antipathies that brothers and sisters inherit or reinvent, and it did the trick with Barbaba and me that week in Drumfoyle. There was plenty of room at the farm, which gave us more emotional leeway than we'd had in the Ford. We also hit a spell of fairly good weather. Above all I was providing handsomely for my sister's amusement, having led her to the heart of Irish life, both present and past—nearby were New Grange and the prehistoric tomb, and Kells with its six High Crosses, and the medieval Castle at Trim; and in Drumfoyle itself we went for walks, or spread blankets on Oona's lawn and had tea and Irish biscuits, and Barbara sketched, while I read Oona's books. One afternoon as we lay in the cold sunlight I told her about Michael.

"How ironic," she said. "A country full of Irishmen, and you come up with one who isn't exactly."

"Maybe this break will help," I said, though Michael Flynn seemed as remote as he'd have been if I'd gone back to America, which in a way I had—by association. Or to put it another way, I'd been turned around; now I was facing in the direction I'd come from.

Seventeen At noon on Friday Barbara and I left Drumfoyle, going straight to the airport; then for the first time in over a week I returned to Fitzwilliam.

"How was the holiday?" asked Dinah.

"Fine, but I'm glad to be back. For some reason," I said, "I'm exhausted." I went into the box room and lit the fire and slowly unpacked. The restoration of my belongings to their accustomed places had a restorative effect on me, and I was beginning to feel somewhat Irish twenty minutes later when Theresa came to my door.

"Madam's been asking for you," she said. "She wants to see you."

"Now?" I was in no mood for an interview with Mrs. Philbin, but Theresa said Madam happened to be free.

She received me in the lounge, seated at her desk with her coat over her shoulders. I was reminded of the day I'd rented the box room, but this time there was no glass of sherry, and I wasn't invited to sit, though nothing else was out of the ordinary. She was lighting a cigarette. She waved the match till it was dead, averting her face charmingly; then with a slightly smug rueful look she said, "I must ask you to leave."

I didn't quite take it in. "The room's mine through August, isn't it?"

She looked at her hands, fingering the rings. "Something's come up."

I said, "What exactly?" All I could think of was Tomás and our late nights, but that had been months ago.

"I've a nephew arriving from Wexford," she said. "He has no place else to stay. I expect you'll find something quickly." She was marvelously in control of herself and the situation. "I hope to have the room by the end of the month, but of course the sooner the better." She waited for me to leave, and when I didn't, she said, "I understand you were on holiday."

I looked her straight in the eye; then I turned and swept out of the room and down the stairs.

"Is everything all right?" Dinah asked. I was trembling with anger and surprise. I shook my head and dashed into the box room; Dinah followed me, saying, "It's about the flat, isn't it? Mrs. Philbin wants it, doesn't she? Last week Theresa told me she mentioned it, but I didn't really believe she'd pull something like that!"

There was a knock at the door, and Theresa came in, her

little black eyes fierce and frightened. "She had no right to do it!"

That the situation was common knowledge made it real, and I was momentarily disheartened; then suddenly I felt better, for everyone was obviously on my side. "Well," I said, "if she needs the room she needs it, and that's that."

"She doesn't need it at all," Theresa said and then bit her lip, but the grievances of the years boiled over: "There's a psychiatrist wants this as his consulting rooms. He's willing to give her six guineas for it."

I looked around the flat, picturing someone stretched out on the daybed, telling his troubles to someone else seated in the wicker armchair. It seemed no more suitable for that purpose than it had seemed the night Liam and Tomás came back there with a half dozen stout. It was, at best, a place in which to make do, and I'd seen enough of Dublin to know I needn't have settled for that. "Cheer up," I said. "I'll find another place soon."

"Till you do," said Dinah, "why don't you come stay with me?"

I got a mental picture of a day among the huge dark chairs and tables and chests at Dinah's, and the picture didn't appeal to me. I said, "I'll certainly keep it in mind."

Dinah gritted her teeth. "I wouldn't have dreamed she'd stoop so low!"

I said, "Neither would I." But this sounded as if I'd suspected Mrs. Philbin of some other sort of treachery, when in fact my mistake partly lay in having failed to take into sufficient account the depth and variety of response that a given situation can bring into play among the people concerned. "I mean it never occurred to me that she had anything in for me," I said. "She's always been nice enough."

"That's what burns me up! I can't stand double dealing!" Dinah's sympathy was of the purest—wholehearted, with a solid basis in principle, and overflowing with the desire to help. "Look, Ann," she said, "come to supper tonight. I'll ring Molly, and we'll put our heads together and see if we can work something out."

When she and Theresa left, I put on my coat and set off for the mews. Spring seemed to be having a relapse into winter that day. There was a strong wind, and I felt myself to be unfairly up against the elements and everything else as I turned into the lane. Daisy was hauling her bicycle out through the wicket door. "Guess what," I said. "I've been evicted."

"I wish I could say the same. When you see the house you'll clear off the way I am." And she rode away.

Inside the mews there was the air of neglect that can make the most comfortable house seem squalid. "Is that you, Bel?" Oona called from upstairs.

"No, it's me," I said and went up to her room. The fire there had gone out; on the hearth was a tray with a tin teapot, an empty milk pitcher, and half a cup of cold tea.

"Wait'll you hear," she said. "I've been asked to America, a place called—what's wrong?" she broke off. "You look in very bad form." I told her why, and she sat up. "I knew that one would try something." Oona had no compunctions about saying "I told you so," but she made it sound as if by not having been convincing she shared the blame. "I should never have let you get mixed up with her. How much time did she give you?"

"Nothing specific, but I'm going to get out right away."

"No, you're not. You must tell her you can't possibly leave for another month at least." I asked what good that would do, and Oona said, "It'll embarrass her. People like Stella Philbin are never as cheeky as they make out. By the way," she added, "what were you paying for the place?" I told her, and she closed her eyes. "Robbery!"

"A pound of that was for the rates."

"Rates!" she exploded. "You know what that is, don't you?"

"The electricity?"

"Not at all—what it amounts to is you were helping pay her taxes."

"Of all the nerve!"

"She mustn't get away with it," said Oona.

Molly Corcoran took more or less the same line. When I got to Dinah's that evening I found them having the time of their lives, thrashing out my situation. "Call her bluff," said Molly. "Make her throw you out and see how she likes it."

"Why give her the satisfaction?" said Dinah.

"Don't be so bloody English," said Molly.

"English my eye—I'm only being logical."

"Same difference," Molly said.

The law of diminishing returns applies to talking things over, and by the time I got back to the box room I was more unsettled than I'd been that morning after Mrs. Philbin gave me her news. I was sitting by the fire trying to sort things out when Tony stopped by. "What's this I hear?" His big kind face filled with anger and concern, as I confirmed the news Theresa had given him. "What sort of cock-and-bull story were you handed?" he asked.

"Supposedly she wants the room for her nephew, but Theresa told me a psychiatrist's going to set up an office here."

"By God, that's what she needs, a live-in head doctor." Tony swore quietly. "Well," he said, "what'll you do now?"

"Stay on till I find someplace else."

"Clear out, why don't you?" he said. "Let her have her flat."

I said, "It's not that simple."

Moving is a lot of trouble, and besides I was attached to the box room, the scene of my initiation into Dublin life. I knew I'd mourn the loss of this frame of reference and I was daunted by the thought of recreating something of the kind in a different setting where, despite the effort I'd expend, life wouldn't be quite the same. But then there was Michael— mightn't a new flat give things a new and interesting twist? Or would it only destroy the complicated mix of time and place that fosters love? I hadn't made up my mind, when one morning that week he popped in on me unannounced. It was eleven thirty; the door opened, and there he was, looking different for some reason that I couldn't immediately put my finger on. "Can you give me lunch?" he asked.

I said, "How did you get in?"

"One of the dentist's patients was leaving." He took off his jacket. He was wearing a white shirt and a tie—that was the difference.

I said, "How about eggs?"

"Eggs will do. I've got news for you."

"I've got news, too—I have to leave here."

"Oh? You can come out to me if you like." The offer was a bit too perfunctory to be attractive; it was also conditional. "Till you find another place." He followed me over to the stove and stood there as I went about scrambling some eggs.

"What's your news?" I asked.

"I'm up for a job with the Arts Council. I have an interview there this afternoon."

It's hard to talk and make a success of cooking, but Michael didn't seem to notice or care that the eggs I served him were overdone. He ate them in three bites; then he said, "Come and lie down with me."

I said, "You'll muss your nice suit."

"I won't be hired for my tailoring."

"What does it depend on?"

"Connections," he said. "I had lunch with the people in the big house next to mine, and a fellow there who was on the committee offered to put my name up. We'll soon see if he's as important as he made himself out."

As I lay holding him and listening to him I felt a little cheated—my own troubles had got brushed aside. Not that I hadn't already had ample commiseration, and I got more of the same when Jim Larkin called the next day. "You'll not go back to America, will you?" he asked, and when I told him not yet, he said, "Things aren't so bad then. And there's plenty of flats in Dublin, sure there are."

"Not where I want to live."

"If you're going to move, sometimes a complete change is best. You might like to try this side of the city. I could ask my landlady if she knows of anything; then I could take you around." Probably because it was a step I felt in very little danger of following through on, I agreed.

That afternoon I was having a conference with Oona at Bewley's. I got there early and had ordered tea, when John Hogan came and tapped me on the shoulder. "May I?" he asked and he sat down, saying, "How are you getting on, Ann?" As I told him I felt myself getting angry in a slightly artificial way—my original anger having worn off—and the artificiality felt obvious. When I finished, John nodded, rather solemnly and said, "Of course, there's a certain kind of person who isn't to be trusted under any circumstances."

"I certainly know that now."

"Well, you wouldn't want to be too good a judge of character. You'd always be exercising the faculty," he said. "That's the Irish vice."

"One of them."

"Turned against us, have you? Sooner or later everybody does. What did it to you?"

I had a hard time finding a word that wouldn't be a direct insult and finally I settled on, "The harshness."

"You don't mean the weather?"

"That, too," I said.

"Still, people in the States must sometimes needle each other a bit."

"A bit."

"And anyway that's not what makes the difference in life. Good health is the thing."

"And good luck."

"Ah no, give me adversity. It's a great developer of the soul."

"Mine feels musclebound."

There was an edge to this conversation that gave me the feeling John believed I'd spurned him. Though I actually hadn't, events had settled my feelings so firmly elsewhere, that I was glad when Oona turned up. "Let's move to another table," she suggested, but John said he had to leave and he did. Nora put more water into the teapot and swished it around; then she asked for another cup and poured us each some tea.

"I have a plan," I said. "I've decided to subtract from my final rent those extra pounds she charged me for the rates."

But the reason we'd met wasn't uppermost in Oona's mind at the moment. "Oh Ann," she said, "I'm in despair over Annabel. This morning she took an hour and a half getting herself off to school, and three quarters of that was in the tub. The hot water, and the soap she uses! And then three towels completely soaked when she's through! If I didn't let it bother me I suppose she'd grow out of it. This way I'm probably ramming it into her character, but it drives me mad." She took a drink of tea and shuddered. "It's stone cold. We might as well move on." I paid the bill, and we went out onto Grafton Street. "You wouldn't ever walk through Brown Thomas with me?" she asked. "I'm desperate for a new handbag." Hers had a broken clasp that she was always clutching, but the bags we went and examined were all too expensive or not the right shade of brown. I led her over to the sweaters, and after that we went upstairs and looked at coats, and I came across a black velvet raincoat I'd seen in *Vogue*, but that year trench coats were coming back.

"I'd be out of it in this," I said to Oona.

"What's not all the rage is sometimes better value," she said. "The thing everyone wears one year is dated the next."

We went downstairs to the basement and looked at the French saucepans, the English dishes, the Irish lace and linen; Oona bought two facecloths. By the time we stepped out onto Duke Street it was four o'clock, and she said, "Let me just leave in my briefcase at the National Library." It took twenty minutes to stroll over there, arrange with the clerk to keep an eye on the desk, and then to discuss library traffic with him. Back on the street Oona said, "Now Ann, there must be loads

of flats in Dublin. If only we knew where to look." We walked
up Kildare Street and into the Green. Since morning the sun
had been threatening to come out, and on this as yet unfilled
promise, people were sitting in deck chairs and lying around
on the grass. Oona and I stopped at the bridge to watch the
children fishing; then we followed the main path out onto
Leeson Street, where she had a brainstorm. "Tom Wynne
used to live in Pembroke Street. The house was the sort that's
all flats. Let's just go down there and see if I recognize the
place."

Three times we walked up and down Pembroke Street;
finally I said, "Let's call it a day." Though we'd accomplished
nothing, the afternoon seemed successful. Oona always made
you feel that whatever was wrong wasn't a catastrophe—certainly nothing that couldn't be improved by a cup of tea, a
long walk, and a conversation.

Jim Larkin's landlady came up with a room for me to
look at in one of the houses among that dreary network of
attached villas that I'd passed with Barbara on the way in
from the airport. Very North side of the city this house was
with its wrought-iron fence and lace curtains. The woman
who let us in reminded me of a blond Theresa though she
lacked Theresa's reserve. "Ah," she said, "Mrs. O'Malley's
gentleman and his friend. I'm Mrs. Snow. I was expecting
you a bit earlier, but what harm? I'd nothing to do all afternoon only wait around for you." The house was immaculate
and cluttered; bits of crochet, artificial flowers, china dogs
and shepherdesses were everywhere you looked. Mrs. Snow
led us up a steep flight of stairs and down a corridor to a door
which she threw open saying, "There now!" It was a big
dingy room painted light green and hung with faded litho-
graphs of Dublin landmarks—the Four Courts, the Customs
House, the Bank of Ireland. "It's southern exposure," she said,
"though that won't impress you. You've all the sunshine you
like in America. You and your lovely slim figures! I suppose
it's the swimming and the tennis keep you that way."

A husky man with a wild head of hair came up the stairs. Mrs. Snow called, "Good afternoon, Mr. Hayes!" and he murmured something over his shoulder, darting into the room across the hall. "A commercial traveler, away most of the time," said Mrs. Snow. "I suppose that's what makes him keep to himself, but I don't think that's best for people, do you? You get odd and set in your ways if no one's there to give you a land now and again." As we went back downstairs, she ran through the other tenants: "There's Mr. Casey who teaches in the national school; Miss Riordan who has a good position at Clery's in home furnishings and gives me the use of her discount, whenever I buy anything for the house. The room we were looking at used to belong to Mr. MacGinnis who played violin with the *Radio Eireann* Symphony. I love the violin. Sometimes of a Sunday I'd invite Mr. MacGinnis to give a recital in the front parlor. And now he's off to London!" She gave a brisk sigh. "There was no future with the symphony, so he said, and if ever a lad deserved a future it was Mr. MacGinnis. The loveliest young man—but there you are! What do you think of the room?"

"How much is the rent?" I asked.

"Fifteen shillings." She threw her shoulders back in a gesture that was half defiance and half plea. "You'll not get near as good value for the money anyplace else in Dublin." I said I'd have to think about it, and she told me, "I'll need to know quickly. There's a gentleman very keen to have it, a supervisor at the Electricity Supply Board."

"Thank you for showing it to us," said Jim.

When we were back on the doorstep, I turned to him and said, "You know, I used to dream of living in a house like that."

"Dreams are marvelous, aren't they?" he said. "Just so long as they don't come true."

Eighteen In the end I found myself a flat from an advertisement in *The Irish Times*. The house was on Auburn Avenue on the borderline between Ballsbridge and Donnybrook, and the bedsitter was self-contained with a kitchenette, a private bath, and a private entrance. The girl who lived there had broken her leg and gone home to recuperate, and her mother showed me the place. "Maura's coming back in September, when college reopens, but till then we'd like to keep the flat occupied."

If I were without a flat in the fall, I knew I'd be minus one reason for staying on in Ireland, and this made me find fault. "It's a bit farther from town than I'm used to."

"The number-ten bus stops at the corner. Or you could easily walk from here." I asked if there was access to a telephone, and she said, "Upstairs in the hall. Cook answers it and she's very good about messages. Though I ought to warn you—you might run into Mrs. Hynes who owns the house. She's a bit off her head. Cook's really her keeper." Like the whores in Fitzwilliam Square, this struck me as a side of life with diverting or instructive possibilities. "By the way, I'm Eileen Clarke," said the woman, offering me her hand.

It was a common surname in Ireland, not sufficient cause for me to believe I was shaking the hand of fate, but that was how I felt. "My name is Clarke, too!"

"Let me take you up and introduce you to Cook."

There was an inside door opening on a flight of stairs leading to the first floor. When we'd got halfway there, a dog began barking hysterically and he met us upstairs, snapping and dancing around our legs. "Off with you, Bobby!" said Mrs. Clarke. "Bad dog! Shoo!" He backed off, looking put out and frightened, still barking and snapping.

At the front end of the hall was the telephone, a pay phone. Near the head of the stairs was a door with a panel of smoked and clear glass, and through it could be seen an old woman in a maid's uniform. Her face was plain, and her gray hair had come loose from a bun at the back to hang in damp, stringy tendrils about her face. She saw us and opened the door, shouting, "Do you be wanting something?"

"She's a bit deaf," Mrs. Clarke said to me; and to Cook, "This is Miss Clarke who's going to take over the flat!"

"Another of the daughters?" Cook asked.

"No relative at all," I said.

"Fancy!" said Cook. "And the same name!"

"That'll make it easy to remember," I suggested. Or would it only be confusing? I glanced in the direction of the telephone just as a door at that end of the hall opened. A face peered out as Bobby slid through the opening; then the door banged shut.

"She'll be wanting to know what's going on," said Cook.

Mrs. Clarke and I went back downstairs where she gave me a set of keys, and I paid her a week's rent. It was only three pounds.

At ten o'clock on the morning I left her house, Mrs. Philbin received me one last time in the lounge. "Leaving now, are you?" she said from the desk where she was going over some bills. "It's been a pleasure having you here, though we didn't see much of one another, did we?" I took the house key from my coat pocket and placed it on the desk. "You could have left that with Ta," said Mrs. Philbin and dropped it in a drawer. "You've found another flat, have you?" I told her where it was, and she said, "You'll be near the show grounds, the Royal Dublin Society where the horse show's held."

"I'm not interested in horses," I said, reaching into my pocket for the envelope there; on it I'd printed in large, arresting letters: *April rent—minus 8 pounds overcharge for rates.* I handed it over, and she studied it for a minute and then covered it with her hand. The knuckles and veins stood out sharply; the rings on her long fingers looked encrusted, the growth of half a lifetime of vanity, yes, but of disappoint- ment and tragedy as well. I remembered what she'd said the day I rented the box room—"It'd be nice for a change, having a young woman in the house." But Stella Philbin was some- one who'd rather not have had a younger and apparently more fortunate woman anywhere near her. She looked at me now with eyes full of dislike and distrust.

"Will you please explain this?" she said.

"You had no right to make me pay into your taxes."

She thought this over; then shrugging, as if the whole business were too undignified for words, she said, "I think you'd better leave."

Oona was driving me to the new flat. I was to be down- stairs at ten fifteen, but it was quarter to eleven by the time Daisy rang the doorbell. My books and dishes and my new clothes had overflowed into two cardboard cartons, but with Dinah and Theresa to help, we got everything out to the car in one trip. Dinah said, "This isn't goodbye, Ann. We'll be seeing heaps of each other."

Theresa was wringing her apron. "It's a shame," she kept saying. "You oughtn't to be leaving like this. It's a terrible shame." The front door was open, and I could see Queen Maeve sitting disdainfully erect in the hall, as if she'd been dispatched by her mistress to keep an eye on things; then Dinah's phone began to ring. That sound had been the theme song of life for me in Fitzwilliam Square—an unsatisfactory life in some ways but my own which I finally understood that I was being forced to relinquish.

"I must get that," Dinah said with a catch in her voice. "Cheerio, Ann."

"You've got my new telephone number," I reminded Theresa.

"I'll give it to anyone that rings!" The look on her face spoke of lingering hopes for Tomás. "You must promise to come back and visit us."

"I will, I definitely will," I said as I stepped away from the front door, knowing I'd never see the inside of Twenty Fitzwilliam Square again.

"How did it go?" Oona said, as I got into the car.

"She took it without a word," I said. "I just hope she doesn't decide to sue me."

"Are you mad?" said Daisy.

"She hasn't the grounds," Oona said. "Or the wit." She shifted gears, and we shot forward.

"Mind the crossing, mother!"

"God—I very nearly hit that fellow!" We swung onto Leeson Street, crossed the Canal Bridge and went down Morehampton Road to Auburn Avenue: That was how close the new flat was—a five-minute drive from the old one. But it was a twenty-minute walk; I'd timed it twice. As we pulled up in front of the house, the dog went into a frenzy, and Mrs. Hynes began screaming. Oona said, "At least no one will be able to steal in on you."

Daisy and I unloaded my belongings; then I saw them off and began the process of taking possession. The flat was damp but it had a three-bar electric heater as well as a gas fire. I turned them both on and unpacked my clothes and put them away in the huge closet. When I finished this I tried all the furniture. The tartan-upholstered armchairs were slightly stiff but in first-class condition, though I took the several rings on the table by the window as leave not to worry about spoiling things. In the bathroom I washed my hands and examined my face in the mirror—I looked nonplussed by all this new luxury. The kitchen had an electric cooker with four burners and a real oven, plus an electric kettle. There was a small refrigerator, and the built-in cabinets contained a full set of dishes complete with soup tureen.

I made myself a cup of tea and sat down at the table by the window. It was a cloudy day, but I was struck by how bright the place was—sunlight had seldom penetrated the box room. At memory of that pleasant gloom, lost forever, I was beginning to feel sorry for myself, and the knock on my inside door came just in time. "You're wanted on the phone!" Cook shouted.

It was Beatrice Driscoll. "What did *you* do? I rang Fitzwilliam, and the girl said you'd had to leave!" As I explained, Beatrice kept going, "Uh-huh," until I realized she had something else on her mind, and I asked what it was. "Are you by any chance free three weeks from this Friday?" she said. "Neil and I are going down to Kilkenny for the day, and I wondered if you could stay with Tricia. I realize this is awful long notice, but Tricia asked for you specially."

I waited till Sunday; then I called Michael. "I've been thinking of you," he said. "In fact I was going to ring."

I said, "I've left Fitzwilliam. I found a much better flat." As if my good fortune had brought on or were due to some general turn for the better in people's affairs, I went ahead and asked, "Did you get that job?"

He said, "No, but I have another angle."

I remembered his hopeful expression and his elation the day he'd dropped in on me; then I remembered holding him. "What sort of angle?" I asked.

"Come out and I'll tell you, and you can tell me about your new flat."

"It'd make more sense for you to come and see it." As I said this, the door at my back opened and I could feel the old madwoman's eyes on me.

"Wouldn't you rather be here? It's a fine enough day."

"All right," I said and hung up. I was nervous as I turned away from the phone, but madness though terrifying to contemplate is only disturbing to confront.

"Have we met somewhere?" the old woman said. She was wearing a floor-length black lace dress and a black mantilla. I told her I'd taken the flat downstairs, and she cast an angry glance in the direction of the kitchen. "She tells me nothing!"

I could see Cook's bony shoulders, her stringy white hair; when she looked up from what she was doing, her simple

face wore a look of such pure resignation and such blame-
lessness that I felt a rush of anger towards her mistress,
blameless though she, too, might possibly be—blameless but
at the moment furious. She drew back into her front room
and slammed the door in my face.

During the bus ride I kept running over this bizarre
encounter, making it into a story for Michael—to cheer him
up was how I thought of it, but it turned out I'd misread his
mood on the phone; it also turned out that he'd changed the
furniture around—cleaned up the spare room and moved the
bed in there, bought a secondhand sofa and an armchair and
made the all-purpose room a proper parlor. "Well," he said,
"what do you think?"

"It's a great improvement." But I felt disoriented as I
went and tried the sofa. "It's like a different place."

He sat down in the easy chair and said, "I ran into a
friend of yours last week, someone by the name of Liam
MacMahon."

I had a chilling sense of change, of a regrouping, as in
those children's games where the players repeatedly switch
places, and you must keep moving or be out. "Dublin *is* a
small city," I said.

"What a marvelous rogue that fellow is!"

I said, "He was far too cynical for me."

"You don't understand, he's a type."

I picked up the cardigan I'd just taken off and put it back
on. "Where did you meet him?" I asked.

"At a party, a great stew of people that bubbled up one
night when the pubs closed. All Dublin was there."

I shook my head and said, "Those parties."

"I met a fellow from *Radio Eireann* who offered me a job.
I have an interview Monday week."

The *Radio Eireann* people I'd met with Tomás were the
ones who drank the most and they were indistinguishable in
my mind—one red face, one pair of bloodshot eyes. It was
hard to imagine Michael among them; he was so self-con-
trolled and so aloof. "What sort of job would it be?" I asked.

"Writing scripts for cultural programs."

I got up and closed the French windows. Earlier in the day there'd been rain; then at half past two the sun appeared and ever since it had come and gone fitfully. One minute everything was as bright as if it were under a glaze; the next minute everything looked gray. In this sort of weather the mountains were at their best, their most mysterious, but I found the sight of them disquieting. At the moment I needed a more level and open view of the world—some simple meadow that would have made life seem more equable.

"How lucky you were to get in with that crowd," he said.

"I'm surprised you never ran up against them before."

"My experience was different from most Dubliners'," he reminded me.

I went to the desk, gave the snow-scene paperweight a shake, and watched the blizzard swirl around the cozy cottage inside. "Would work like that leave you time for your book?" I asked.

"I'd have to make the time, but it'd be well worth it. Those jobs are scarce, and when you get one you're set for life."

I returned to the sofa, this time to the end nearest him. "When I rang you today I ran into my mad landlady," I said.

"Where would you say that crowd usually goes—Neary's or MacDaid's?"

"It all depends," I said. "She was dressed for a Papal audience."

"The pubs are as specialized as the medical profession."

"She has a horrible little dog that acts mad, too."

"Small dogs are all silly. Mastiffs are the thing to have."

"And then there's Cook."

"Let me have the phone number," he finally said, reaching for his notebook and pencil.

I gave it to him, remembering the night of Nora's party— how he'd walked me home and carefully noted the old number in that same book. How little I'd cared for him then and how much I cared now. This impressed itself on me not as a steady growth of feeling but as a wild tangle that in the course of the afternoon I broke through, though at the time I felt I was getting it to go in the direction I wanted—it's in the nature of the beginning of the end that the process should at first appear reversible; but I hadn't yet acquired the discipline, discovered in myself the powers of dissemblance that sometimes can, in fact, turn such things around. We were lying in the newly designated bedroom; I looked at him and said, "You know how much I love you."

He was startled and then in a succession just slow enough for the stages to be distinguishable and appear deliberate: tender, rueful and cautious. "Ann dear," he said and sat up, plucked a primrose from the glass on the table, and put it in my hair. "You must be hungry," he said. "Shall we eat something?"

Nineteen   The dampness of the new flat almost canceled out all its virtues. During the day I didn't mind, but to get comfortable in the evening I had to plug in the electric heater, light the gas fire, and sit between the two. I'd soon feel a little too warm and I'd have to take off my tights and then cover my bare legs with my skirt to keep them from getting blotched, and that was the stage I'd reached one evening when my bell rang. I went to the door and opened it before I remembered I was barefoot—a priest was standing there holding his hat. He had thin gray hair, a thin face, thin lips. He'd have looked severe except for his eyes which had a friendly though, on account of the thickness of his glasses, slightly faraway expression. His voice had the same quality, interested but remote. "I'm sorry," he said. "I've caught you by surprise. I'm Father Broderick from the church down the street."

Upstairs the dog began to bark. I raised my voice and said, "Come in, Father."

"You've a good protector up there!" he shouted.

"Or an enemy." Overhead there was the sound of scrambling and of Mrs. Hynes screaming. The priest and I stood looking at each other till it died down; then he put his hat on the table, pulled out a chair, said, "May I?" and sat down. As I slid into my shoes, he looked at his own feet and cried, "Here am I still with my bicycle clips on!" He bent over and unfastened them. "I'm not used to going around on the old bike. I had a car at my last parish." He folded his arms across his chest and crossed his legs at the ankles. He looked more at home than I did as I sat down at the table, and it occurred to me that he was probably used to putting people at ease in their own houses. "We try to call on all the parishioners at least once during the year," he said.

I told him my name. "But I wouldn't call myself a parishioner," I said.

"You've landed yourself a nice neat flat anyway. It's very compact, though you've not much room for your things. Still you're probably better off—the more space you have the more stuff you accumulate. I've two big rooms at the rectory and I can hardly fit in all my books and papers, plus the bits of furniture my mother left me." I said that I didn't know priests owned furniture, and he told me, "We do indeed. I've two big easy chairs, a nice desk, and a chest of drawers. And of course, the piano, my one indulgence. When I was a boy I had an idea of doing something in that line, but you have to be top dog in this country to get any sort of chance."

"That bothers me a lot," I said.

Father Broderick smiled. "Now it's your turn. Tell me why you wouldn't call yourself a parishioner." I said that I was there temporarily, having been put out of Mrs. Philbin's, and he pretended to be shocked. Behind the pretense was the readiness to revise first impressions, and when I told him it wasn't my fault (and thus something for him to deal with) he looked relieved. "Are you studying in Dublin?" he asked, and I said I was supposed to be. "And what are you supposed to be studying?" I told him, and he scratched his head—a close-cut, well-shaped head and not, I'd have said, a bookish one. "You must be homesick all this way and on your own. Or have your people come over?" I mentioned Barbara's visit. "That must have been a great old reunion," he said. "What about the parents?"

I wondered what to say and how much and decided to tell him as much as possible. I couldn't help feeling he'd come out of the night for just that purpose. "I don't think my mother would have liked it here," I said, "because I think my father would have liked it a little too much." He pretended not to know I was getting at anything, and so I came right out with it. "My father bets on horses, and I wouldn't like to see him in a country full of betting parlors."

"So that's the story."

When told, it had a melodramatic ring that I found myself shrugging off. "You must hear an awful lot of that."

"And you seem to've got the better of it anyway, off on your own like this."

It was all very well for me to dismiss my story, but should a priest be allowed to do that? "I don't think you ever get the better of your biography," I said.

The look he gave me was kind in a professional way. "No matter what happens in life, the important thing is to stay close to God and go to confession and communion as often as possible. You know that, don't you, Ann?"

I hesitated—more for effect, I think, than from a reluctance to confide in this nice priest. At any rate what I said next had elements of both drama and anticlimax: "I haven't been to confession in a long time."

"What kept you away?" he asked and then lifted his head, as if he were just seeing the light, as if it hadn't been shining in his face for the last minute or two. "The boy friend,

I suppose." I nodded, and he asked, "Are you going to get him to marry you?"

"He'll marry an Irish girl." It was the first time I'd said that to myself or to anyone else.

"Then drop him. Don't waste your time," said the priest. "And make it definite." As if to set this example, he himself took another tack. "I hope you've made a load of friends since you've been in Dublin. It's best to see plenty of people, and the Irish are good folk when you get to know them." He looked at his watch. "God in heaven, I'm behind in my evening's calls!" He got up and came around the table and brought me to my feet. "Would you like to go to confession?" he asked.

I said, "I thought I just did."

"Let's do the job properly. I'm in the box on Saturday from twelve till one and from four till six and then again from half seven till nine at night. That gives you a choice in case you're planning on seeing the fellow."

"I'm seeing someone else," I said.

"That's the girl!" he cried. "There's plenty of fish in the sea!"

Father Broderick was a good-natured and, within the limits of his duties, an understanding man. It couldn't have been easy or enjoyable spending your spare time visiting people who probably didn't expect or welcome you, and I didn't want him to feel that in my case he'd failed to do his job, nor did I want to have him try again. Besides, virtue is a seductive notion—to put on "the new man" and throw off the sense of being out of phase that conduct formerly and sometimes still thought of as wrong can inspire. Furthermore, the priest offers you a way out of unsatisfactory situations, and I thought this might be a relief; I was weary of the impasse that was Michael Flynn's passion for Ireland, though at the back of my mind I was aware, too, that you sometimes need only give up on a thing for it to come right.

Father Broderick's church was unprepossessing, but as I knelt down there that Saturday, the huge white altars and garish statues put me in the spirit of the step that no matter how little you expected of it, always turned out to be deflating. Only a handful of people had showed up at noon. Two children headed the line outside Father Broderick's box, and they were in and out in nothing flat; then an old woman took her turn, and for ten minutes some labored rigmarole of scruple came through my side of the box. When I heard him giving her absolution, I realized I was a little nervous. Confession is, apart from anything else, an intimate act though it takes place in the probable absence of the factors on which anything of an intimate nature depends—compatibility, common interests, a congenial setting, and time for all this to take effect. And so I wasn't surprised, after I told the priest who I was, to have him get right down to business. "I suppose you've been missing Mass, Ann."

"No, I haven't," I said. It's not that a half hour of prescribed prayer makes everything add up, but the mere attempt at such a thing is some comfort. Besides, I like the ritual; it satisfies my sense of order and my faith in the force of habit—its power unexpectedly to redeem all the time it otherwise eats up.

Father Broderick said, "All we really have to worry about then is your man. Are you going to break up the affair?"

"There's not much to break," I had to admit.

"You'll feel better for making it definite."

The firm purpose of amendment—you had to be careful about that. Once you let yourself promise to do or not do something, you couldn't go back on the promise without despising yourself. "I'll probably be going home soon," I said.

"Remember how we talked about friends—you must have plenty to do, you must keep busy. What about this afternoon?" I told him I was going out to Howth. "You're early for the rhododendrons," he said, "but still and all Howth's lovely. Run along now. Enjoy yourself." Not till I was outside did I realize he hadn't given me a penance to

say. I looked at my watch. It was half past twelve; I was meeting Jim Larkin at one, and a bus was coming.

Irish buses don't always come to a complete standstill,
and I stumbled getting on board that one, though my shoes
were partly to blame—eight months of Irish rain had stiffened and stretched those black patent-leather slingbacks.
They were the first thing Jim Larkin noticed when I met him
at the G.P.O. "I wonder will those little pumps be comfortable," he said, and I realized why after forty-five minutes
and another bus ride. The country road where we got off led
to a headland of daunting proportions.

I said, "I was picturing some pretty seaside village." On
the phone he'd said we'd go for a walk and then have prawns
at the Abbey Tavern.

"That's at the other end," he said now, looking back at
my shoes. "Maybe we ought to turn around."

Common sense, like instinct in animals, is rooted in the
physical world, and failing to be sensible can be as demean-
ing as any pratfall. The only thing to do is pick yourself up
and keep going. I said, "Come on," and reached into my coat
pocket for a headscarf.

"I like that little scarf. It suits you," he said. "Yellow's
your color, though red's most exciting on women—red or
black. There's glamour in the harshness. Yellow's got a glamour of its own though, especially with dark hair like yours."

I wasn't paying much attention to all this—Howth Head
was rough going in those shoes. The narrow dirt path was
full of rocks, and the only intimations of the sea were the
gulls dipping and soaring overhead. They were the only signs
of life as well. "This reminds me of *Wuthering Heights*," I
said.

"Only I'm not your Heathcliffe," he said sadly.

We struggled on in a silence I meant to be an accusation
that I then couldn't in all honesty sustain. "What's the yellow
plant?" I asked. For I knew it wasn't his fault that I was wearing the wrong shoes—I should have asked him what to expect.

"They call it broome in England. Here we call it gorse."

He picked a branch for me to smell; it had a fragrance like melon and daffodils combined, sweet and strong. "It's a pity Molly Bloom's rhododendrons aren't out," he said. "Do you remember? It was here she delivered her famous piece."

The lasciviousness in question was only literary, but it pinpointed the uneasiness I'd begun to feel. I said, "I certainly pictured Howth differently." Up ahead stood a solitary bench that from a distance looked absurd—out there in the middle of nowhere—but when we reached it and sat down I discovered that the bench was placed strategically to show off a panorama that struck me as essentially Irish, contradictory—vivid and somber, severe and romantic, rugged and unearthly. There was the sea now, and a pair of satellite islands offshore.

"The largest is called Ireland's Eye. The other's Lambay Island." He reached over to pick up a stone and began tossing it from one hand to the other. "Do you think will you ever come back to Dublin?"

"You make me feel as if I've already left."

"I'd try and keep you here myself if I thought there was the slightest chance."

"What's that noise?" I'd been aware of it for some time and thought it was a ringing in my ears, maybe something to do with climbing, but now the sensation I had was of ringing all around me.

He dropped the stone and grabbed me by the hand, saying, "I want to show you something!"

What folly—going to that godforsaken spot with someone who knew I didn't love him. Play for time, I told myself as I stepped forward. Be calm, just go along. That I'd been to confession struck me as significant of I didn't like to think what, and I remembered I hadn't got a penance, I hadn't even made a firm purpose of amendment. Too late, I thought—now it wouldn't count. We were at the cliff's edge, when he let go of my hand and cried, "There!" A living crust of gulls was clinging to the rockface. "Those are the nests!"

I took a step back and said, "For heaven's sake."

Safety is a factor in happiness if not in love, and the sense of being out of danger buoyed me up for the rest of the walk—from that point on it was downhill anyway to the pretty seaside village I'd been expecting in the first place. Couples in suits and coats were strolling along the promenade, or leaning on the rails, looking out over the water. We joined them for a few minutes; then we went to the Abbey Tavern and sat by the fire and had the whiskeys and shared the plate of prawns. "Days when you don't plan much are marvelous," he said.

I said, "Aren't they," and it occurred to me that with Michael I'd probably have qualified my agreement in an effort to make it more interesting. It's this, the depreciation of self, that makes love so costly; and the self-possession that someone you don't love brings out in you is often enough to make you reconsider, but when I looked at Jim Larkin and asked myself, "Why not him?" the answer came readily: he was too raw, too much work needed to be done on him.

Twenty Upheaval in your own life makes it vital that the rest of the world stay on an even keel, and it upset me the day I went over to the mews and found the whole place turned upside down. Daisy was in the courtyard, beating carpets, wearing shorts with a torn blue shirt and a black scarf around her head. She gave me a dark look and said, "Be prepared to make yourself useful."

Oona had been assigned the job of going through her papers, and they were billowing out of the file cabinet, over the desk, and onto the floor; my arrival was the excuse to take a break that she and Annabel had been looking for.

"Daisy's an awful bully," said Annabel with her pretty, put-upon air. She too had tied a scarf around her head, but hers was blue silk and matched her eyes.

"Daisy's a saint," Oona said. "I don't know how she puts up with the rest of us."

Annabel made tea and brought it out back where there was a garden, a perfect bower, with beds of iris and dahlias, and a stone bench under a trellis covered with clematis. A bee began investigating the plate of biscuits, and Oona turned over her saucer on top of them. "Silly fellow," she said, "going after lobster when there's roast beef in those roses."

Annabel stretched out and said, "Tell Ann about the autumn." Then she couldn't resist telling me herself. "Daisy wants us to move down to Drumfoyle in September and live there to save money. She wants to set the mews."

Certain words and phrases—autumn, September, next year, the end, a change in—caused me a kind of suffering that I'm sure is what someone must feel at the diagnosis of some disease that will let you live but in a drastically altered and limited state. I said, "I wouldn't call living in Meath a hardship."

"You're always going on about Ireland," said Annabel. "It's no bloody Eden, you know."

I said, "Isn't it?"

Annabel rolled over and said, "You're hopeless, you Americans. You're all soft on anything that's not your own."

"I ought to pack them off to Italy," said Oona.

I said, "Do whatever makes things easiest for yourself." I didn't like how this sounded but I wasn't sure why, and the remark turned annoyingly in my mind, like a mobile off kilter, till Madeleine came to an upstairs window.

"Don't eat all the biscuits!" she called. "I mean cookies!" And she went into hysterical laughter.

I never got used to the idea that I had an accent nor to having this pointed out, and I was already feeling slightly uncomfortable when Daisy suddenly appeared in the doorway. "Drinking tea, you rotten slobs!" She peeled off her scarf and threw it on the ground. Her curly hair stood up all over her head; her eyes were full of tears of anger. "As for you, Ann Clarke—just because you've nothing to do with yourself doesn't mean the rest of us can lie around all day!"

I sat up straight and said, "I'd be glad to help you, Daisy."

"Ah, don't be such a fool," Annabel said to me. "Daisy's an awful old drudge. Everyone knows that."

Oona said, "We'll finish up tomorrow, Daise. Sit down and have your tea."

"I'm surprised you left me any," said Daisy, but there was a cup and more still in the pot, and we all had another few drops. I couldn't help feeling I'd triggered Daisy's outburst and I briefly lost track of the conversation; when I caught up again, Oona was talking about whether it would be a good idea during the summer for her to stop going to the National Library and work at home instead.

"If only I could get there I'd be all right, but I meet half a dozen people along the way, and someone gets me to stop for coffee, and I lose hours."

I said, "Why not—"

"What?" Oona asked, when I didn't finish the sentence.

I'd been about to suggest that she set aside someplace in the mews as a kind of office, but something had occurred to me that made my mouth go dry: Had I become another Tom Wynne?

To alter the setting people have grown familiar in is to alter their images of each other: this was what I decided the Sunday I made lunch for Molly and Dinah. They couldn't get over the flat. "What a super place!" Molly repeatedly said, and Dinah kept echoing her.

"Simply super!"

"It's a pity you weren't here all along," said Molly. "But then we wouldn't have got to know one another." She took out her cigarettes. "Does anyone mind?"

The chicken salad I'd made was in the tureen, and when

I lifted the lid, Molly let out a gasp. "That's not salad! Salad's lettuce with sliced chicken or ham, or egg and tomato!"

"This is American salad," I said firmly and began serving it.

Molly studied hers, analyzing the ingredients: "Salad cream, chicken, celery—is there apple in it?" she asked. I said no, there wasn't. "Onion?"

"Just chicken and celery."

"Well, it's different," Molly said and began to eat heartily. I'd made a pitcher of iced tea and when I produced it, she gasped again. "Cold tea!"

"Iced," I said. She insisted on having hers with milk, found it undrinkable, and had another glass plain.

"Well, it's different," she said.

"How is Stella getting along without me?" I asked Dinah.

"Actually she spoke about you last week. Well, as a matter of fact we went to the theater together." I thought Dinah was joking but luckily I didn't laugh. She said, "We saw the revue at the Olympia. Quite a good company and rather a pleasant evening on the whole. She's quite charming, you know, when she wants to be. Afterwards Ta gave us supper in the lounge."

To have someone else take advantage of what you've already declined makes the situation look different, and I found myself wishing I'd made the effort to get to know Mrs. Philbin if only that I might still be in Fitzwilliam. Just seeing Dinah and Molly made me so long to be back there that I had to work at being agreeable and kept falling just short of that.

"What sort of house is this?" asked Dinah.

"A madhouse," I said, "literally." And I told them about it. "At least the place is quiet most of the time."

Dinah said, "I always worried about disturbing you."

"More salad?"

Molly declined, but Dinah had another helping. "Just a dab, though it's simply gorgeous." And she proposed a toast in tea. "To a happy couple of months."

"What couple of months?" asked Molly, and Dinah reminded her that was how long I had the flat.

"Oh," said Molly, "then you're off, are you?" She gave a great sigh. "How I envy you, going to New York."

I said, "Why don't you go there yourself?"

"I think Rory'd miss me," she said, "though God knows he does nothing to keep me here. Anyhow, I'd miss him."

"I meant for a visit," I said, though I hadn't—I'd wanted to put Molly on the spot, but she was too generous and too lackadaisical to feel much discomfort there.

"Ah well," she said, "an Irishman is an Irishman is an Irishman. We're all better off staying here if we possibly can."

"I must say, it's never seemed to make the slightest difference to Ireland whether I go or stay," said Dinah, but her position was of course unassailable.

"We Irish," Molly said, "have put up with you English for centuries. I'm afraid we've got in the habit of it."

I'd bought some whiskey for Irish coffee and when I produced the ingredients Dinah said, "Would you like me to do the honors?"

I said, "I think I can manage," but streaks of cream ran down into each coffee as I made it.

"Not to worry," said Dinah, "it'll taste delicious."

"You can't spoil good Irish whiskey," said Molly.

There'd been a real break in the weather—that was the strangest thing. Day after day the sun shone, and the sky was cloudless. I got in the habit of spreading my striped rug in the areaway of the flat and I was sitting there one afternoon, when the dog began to bark. I lifted my head and found Father Broderick wheeling his bicycle up the path. "You've a real little suntrap there," he said.

In the week or so since I'd gone to him to confession I'd once or twice wondered if I should return for a penance; now I wished I had. I couldn't think of why else he might have come by and I put down my book and got respectfully to my feet, but he himself sat down on the blanket. I joined him there, and he said, "Don't tell me you're reading that reprobate Samuel Beckett."

I said, "Beckett's very funny."

"Have you read any Maurice Walsh? He writes wonderful stories about the west of Ireland and the folk there. You'd enjoy his books, I know you would. I've a crowd of them at the rectory that you could borrow." He put the Beckett down, losing my place, I noticed. "How are you getting on, Ann?"

"I know it's silly," I said, "but I feel cut off from things out here."

"The city's lively all right," he said. "I suppose you were always at dress dances and such."

My Dublin life was of an entirely different order, but presumably he'd made a dozen other parish calls since I last saw him and had mixed me up with someone else. To spare him embarrassment I began conforming as best I could to the image of me he'd substituted for the real one, telling him Jim Larkin was taking me to supper that day: "We're going to a place off O'Connell Street where people up from the country have their tea."

"You don't mean the Palace Grill!" He obviously didn't think much of it.

"Supposedly you get lots of food, and it's big and plain and comfortable there." Good Lord, I thought, why go on like this? What difference does it make?

"Well," said Father Broderick, "I mustn't hold you up. I only wanted to see how you're getting on." He got to his feet and took my arm. "Any word on the boy friend?" I shook my head, and he looked pleased. "That's the way!" Michael hadn't rung, and though I'd managed to keep from ringing him, I wasn't perfectly sure what I'd do if I picked up the phone and heard his voice. But I didn't say this to Father Broderick; it was the kind of fine point I'd found him apt to dismiss as he again dismissed Samuel Beckett. "Morbid fellow that! Come by the rectory. I'm on duty every afternoon except Saturday. You can see my digs, and I'll let you have a couple of Maurice Walsh's novels."

On purely descriptive grounds "digs" struck me as the wrong word—no more true to a priest's quarters than "private" was to Twenty Fitzwilliam Square. Furthermore, I had no desire to become a rectory visitor lest I somehow find myself, like my mother, ironing altar cloths and singing in the choir, but I thanked Father Broderick for inviting me and said I'd drop by the following week.

"Mind you do now," he said and he leaned forward and kissed me. My upbringing accustomed me to the affection of priests—that pure spring of feeling, liable suddenly to well up, having no regular outlet—and I wasn't especially upset or even surprised. Still, a kiss isn't a handshake, and I wondered vaguely whether I'd been too familiar with Father Broderick. I remembered the first night he came to the flat when I'd been barefoot. Was that provocative? I knew anything could be. That was why the strategy of dressing down had backfired with Jim Larkin—my old clothes and my own smell might as well have been black velvet and *Arpège*.

I decided to wear what I pleased that evening and in my gray flannel New York dress and some eyeshadow I set off for the G.P.O. When I got there he started in at once: "Are you sure you want to go to the Palace? Do you think you'll like it there? It may not be good enough for you. You might rather have a real meal somewhere."

"Is that what you'd rather do?"

"To be honest," he said, "it doesn't matter to me where we go, so long as I'm off my feet." I noticed then that he was very pale and I asked if he felt all right. "I'll tell you when we're sitting," he said.

But the Palace Grill didn't offer much privacy. It was a huge place, two tiled floors of bare tables set close together. I ordered sausage and egg, and Jim ordered a dish of chips. "Just chips?" I said. "That's not very good for you, if you don't feel well."

He shook his head weakly. "I probably won't eat them anyway."

I looked around and said, "Isn't this nice." The big plain room was full of big, plain people—trenchermen all. The waitresses were exemplary, and we'd hardly given the order when our heaped plates appeared. "All right," I said, lowering my voice, "tell me what's wrong."

"I'm in love," he blurted out.

I groaned inwardly over the impulse that had sent me out in the gray dress and the eyeshadow. "You're really not," I said. "My being foreign is all that attracts you."

"The girl's Irish," he said.

I opened my mouth and then closed it again. It's one thing to make every effort to discourage someone; it's another thing entirely to discover you've accomplished that. "Isn't this awfully sudden?" I said and began eating my sausages.

"I met her at a dance a month ago. She's a nurse at the *Mater*. It was only out of boredom and despair over you that I saw her again, and then we met only twice. The first time we went to the pictures, and the second time I brought her to dinner at Jammet's. I thought it'd be too grand by far for her there, but she took it in stride. Then last Friday she told me she'd met another fellow she likes better." He ate a couple of chips then put down his fork as if he were going to be sick.

I said, "Maybe you'd rather leave."

"Maybe." He didn't protest when I got the bill and paid it, but outside on O'Connell Street he revived a little. "I'd like a drink," he said. "Would you join me?" I didn't think he should be left by himself, and since I seemed to be out of danger from him—or he was from me—we went to the bar next to the Capitol cinema. There he began again on the girl: "She's from Carlow, only a couple of villages from my own village. Her hair is pitch black, and her eyes are the color of gentians."

A real Irish beauty, I said to myself, the original "Dark Rosaleen." I was quite put out by the whole thing and no less so for the lack of real grounds—I'd gone out of my way to neutralize myself and now it served me right to have to sit there listening to him sing someone else's praises. But I began to get bored and to keep my mind from wandering I asked, "Do you think she might just be trying to get you to come across?"

He looked horrified and hopeful at the same time. "You mean she wants me to marry her?"

"Not necessarily. She might be trying to see how far you'd go, just for the sake of it."

"And I might be acting true to form—ringing her up and all. Today I rang her four times," he admitted.

"Give that up for a while and see what happens," I said. "But remember, people like her believe in those things—putting on acts and making you do what they want. And sooner or later what they want is the house, and the furniture, and the dinner parties, and all the rest of it."

"You don't believe in that?" he asked.

I wouldn't have thought that was true, and so it was with a sense of surprise and some dismay that I recognized where I stood with respect to the life I'd described. "I guess I don't. Not really. Or not enough. You couldn't if you ever started thinking very much about it."

"Most people don't think," he said. "They go blindly."

I said, "I wish I could."

"It's far more beautiful to live consciously."

"I don't know if I agree." I did know that if I weren't careful I'd find myself back where I started with him; then it struck me that I'd mind the situation less—being admired is no substitute for being in love, but they're equally habit forming.

I had no particular desire to read the books of Maurice Walsh or to see the inside of Sacred Heart rectory, and three weeks went by before I got myself to that big gloomy red brick building. The doorbell chimes played a tune that sounded vaguely ecclesiastical to me as I waited on the front steps; then a priest on his way out let me into the handsome, paneled hall. A door opened suddenly; Father Broderick stood there in his shirtsleeves. "Much obliged to you, Cormac," he said. "Come in, Ann. It's nice to see you." I followed him into a big sitting room, and he said, "There's the piano." It was a mahogany spinet, polished to a high gloss and placed by the window where it caught the light. "Sit down," he said. "You'll have some sherry, sure you will."

"Lovely," I said, and when he handed me a glass I said it again, "Lovely."

"You weren't expecting anything so presentable, were you?" he asked. Actually I'd tried and been unable to picture the furniture he'd spoken of; it seemed just beyond the imagery that comes to mind at the words "room" or "house," and even when I was sitting in one of his armchairs and looking around, I had the sense of being in some made-up place, like a stage set that would be struck in an hour or two. "It's different for priests in America," he said. "I once spent a summer in Passaic, New Jersey, and the rectory there was nothing like as comfortable as this. Each man had his own bedroom, of course, but there was only the common parlor. Very hard on the fellows, I'm sure."

"You'd think it'd be the other way around," I said, "more elaborate there." I didn't see that I'd been tactless till he began to laugh.

"Ah yes, we're backward here in Ireland, there's no denying that." He put down his glass. "Will I play something for you?"

I was expecting Bach or maybe Chopin, but he opened the piano bench on a pile of sheet music, songs with a picture of the vocalist on each cover. The numbers he selected were from that valley between the great popular composers and the powerful rock stars. "My Way," "Hey There!," "Volare," "Venus If You Will"—he had a heavy touch and a weakness for the pedal that made me want to shout, "Stop!" In the midst of this there was a knock at the door. I hoped someone had come to complain but the priest who stuck his head in said, "I'm up in town for the day, Jack, and I thought I'd look in. But I see you're busy."

"I can't stay," I said and started to get up.

Father Broderick looked angry. His face was flushed, and he frowned at me and then at the other priest who began to back off, saying as he left, "I'll call again later."

"I really should go," I said, finishing off my sherry.

Father Broderick left the piano bench and came around behind my chair. "You've been here only a minute or two," he said and he leaned over and covered my breasts with his hands. That scene is like a cinematic freeze-frame in my mind, a sudden illuminating halt to the action, but in reality things went quietly and crazily on, almost as if nothing had happened—I laid down my glass, edged myself off the chair, straightened my skirt, said, "Thank you for the sherry."

"Is there anything you need?" The inflection in his voice was suspiciously spiritual. I'd have ignored it, but he insisted, "Do you want confession?"

"I'll come by the church," I said, taking the lead as we crossed the hall; then I had to wait for him to catch up and open the double-latched rectory door. Sunshine poured in. I started down the front steps, and he called after me.

"Wait! The books! Maurice Walsh!"

I turned and put up my hand to shade my eyes. "That's all right," I said, "I'll get them at the library," and I kept on going.

Glaring sunshine can give an afternoon a look of desolation, and as I went on my way I felt as if I were passing through scenes of destruction—ruined streets, ravaged buildings—till I turned onto Pembroke Road. There in the cold shade I saw a phone box at the corner, told myself that to make what had just happened an excuse for calling Michael would be a kind of cheating, and then went in and dialed his number. As the phone rang and rang, impulse hardened to compulsion and I started walking more or less from one phone box to the next, ending up on Grafton Street. It was the height of the afternoon promenade or crush, but I stuck it out till I got to Brown Thomas. After using the telephone there, I walked upstairs to the café and went in and sat down and ordered tea and scones.

The women at the surrounding tables were the picture of what Jim Larkin meant when he called someone or something "*bourgeois*." Their tweed, the forceful tilt of their sculptured hats, the absorption with which they worked their way through plates of cakes and sandwiches—all this put me off my own tea. I drank half a cup, ate half a scone, and then took the bus back to Auburn Avenue where I went straight upstairs and rang Michael again. As I stood there I heard stealthy sounds behind me, and in hopes that Mrs. Hynes might give up and close her door again, I let the phone ring past the ten times I'd been allowing myself before I replaced the receiver.

She was wearing the black lace dress but no mantilla. Her hair was freshly done, and she'd doused herself with perfume, a floral scent—carnation or rose. She put a finger to her lips beckoning me with the other hand, and lest a refusal provoke her, I followed her into her sitting room. I was instantly reminded of Dinah's, but here there was even more and much showier stuff, of which the showiest piece by far was the immense sideboard arrayed from end to end with a collection of hollow silver: two huge covered platters, a tea and coffee service, a massive punch bowl, a monstrous pair of candelabra. In what previous existence had they been useful or at least used, and how had that Mrs. Hynes carried them off? Grandly, no doubt; there was so much leftover grandeur still in her. "Sit down," she commanded, pointing to the sofa where she joined me, saying, "I have something to show you." But then she fell back into her quandary and asked, "Have we met before?" I reminded her that I lived downstairs, and she cast a vicious look in the direction of the kitchen. "The woman tells me nothing," she said. "Be on your guard, or she'll get hold of you, too." I wondered what had happened in Cook's life and in her mistress's to bring about their awful partnership, what series of events, incredible or routine, had broken the spirit of one and the mind of the other.

Mrs. Hynes reached for my hand and put something there, saying, "I want you to have this." I opened my fingers on an oval mirror, the kind that came with purses when I was a child. One such mirror of mine had a picture of Shirley Temple reproduced on the back, and I wasn't altogether surprised to find a picture on the back of the mirror I'd just been given. "Myself as a girl," said Mrs. Hynes. A coquette: looking flirtatiously at the camera, her white dress all ruffles and ribbons, one hand flashing an open fan, the other hand on her hip with the fingers bent back in an exaggerated come-hither gesture that could only have been self-defeating. "As you can see I was very beautiful," she said. I agreed, and a glimmer of highly reasonable distrust shone momentarily in her dull eyes. "You're good looking, too," she said, "though not as good looking as I was. I had beaux and beaux and beaux. All of them gone now." Her effort to look sad produced a fresh burst of spite. "You must protect yourself," she said. "Your beauty will fade. You'll be at the mercy of others." There was another vicious glance towards the kitchen, followed by an appeal: "Can I trust you?"

I said, "Of course," and armed myself with some mental reservations.

But whatever grudge she'd meant to share slipped her mind. She turned me to the light and studied my face for a minute; then she said, "Don't be too nice. It won't get you anyplace."

I half wanted to see if she could be made to produce a better example of mad wisdom and half wanted to punish someone, anyone, as I said, "You can't go around barking at people."

"Bold," she said. "Be bold." And then her face closed to me, as if in two sentences she'd dispensed the whole of her own store of boldness. Coldly offering me her hand she got to her feet and said, "How kind of you to stop by. You must come again."

Twenty=one "Let's have our tea now, Trish," I said. "I'm getting stiff." For half an hour we'd been crouched on the bank of the pond. "I think the ducks have had enough, too." They'd begun swimming away from us.

"But I still have lots of bread," said Tricia.

"You don't have to finish it all today. Save some for another time."

"But this is a nice day," she pointed out. "Lots of days aren't nice enough."

"True," I said and leaned back on the grass.

"Why don't you feed some?"

"You're better at it than I am." When she put a crust in my hand, I gave it a toss just short of the water, and one diehard duck clambered up onto the bank. Tricia jumped back.

"You did it wrong!" she scolded me.

"I told you I'm not as good as you are." The diehard gobbled up the bread and returned to the pond. "Now you can feed them again," I said, but Tricia had her eye on three or four boys and girls who'd come to fish a little further down the bank. They were typical Dublin children, well-behaved but loud, the boys in short pants that covered the knee, the girls in dresses ridged at the hem—obvious hand-me-downs—and hair ribbons that looked as if they'd been torn from old nylon petticoats.

"Those are very rough children, aren't they?" Tricia complained, and dusting herself off she said, "I'm thirsty. Let's have tea."

The Green was crowded. Every deckchair had an occupant, and there were periodic traffic jams, as the girls in cotton dresses and fellows in shirtsleeves met up with each other on their restless patrol of the paths. Individuals who couldn't or wouldn't pay the price of a chair, lined the benches; or they stretched out on the grass, reading or sunning themselves in solitary comfort or misery. There were pairs of lovers on the grass, too, lying decorously side by side, talking, occasionally touching. The "Garden of Delights," I thought. But with a difference. For one thing these people had their clothes very much on, and no one is clothed so fully as an Irish man or woman. On that warm day, the display of pale arms and legs only brought to mind sweaters and coats and stockings briefly and probably reluctantly left off. Furthermore there was nothing obscure, nothing farfetched about the delights of Stephen's Green. It was, like the city where it was situated, like the country itself, a place of judicious hopes and reasonable pleasures pursued so intensely that they seemed rediscovered.

A pair of African students walked by, and I thought of what a contrast Ireland must be after Nigeria or Sierra Leone or whatever post of missionary priests the Africans had been recruited from. Then the image of Bosch's black men wearing or bearing apples came to me, and I laughed.

Tricia said, "Why are you laughing?"

I said, "I just thought of a picture that reminds me of the Green."

"Can I see it?"

"You wouldn't enjoy it," I said, and she began to pout. "It's a grownup picture," I said.

"With naked people? I've seen naked people pictures. My Mommy lets me look at them in a book."

We reached the place where the paths converged and led to the main gate; the crowd thinned out here, and a couple entering under the great stone arch caught my eye. Their arms were linked, and he was half turned to her in an attitude between concentration and devotion. I told myself I was mistaken and knew it was Michael, knew also that the girl wasn't his sister, cousin, colleague, friend, or acquaintance. We were on top of each other before he recognized me. At that point the girl was looking in the other direction; we could have passed without speaking, and his eyes signaled a desire to do that, but I remembered the old madwoman's words: "You must be bold." I also remembered Father Broderick's suggestion that I'd feel better for a definite break, and under this compelling if questionable inspiration I stopped. As we faced each other I at last appreciated what I'd had to have pointed out and had then only understood—how handsome he was, how fine his gray eyes were, what energy and determination showed in his perfect posture and in his strong voice.

Nodding at Tricia, he said, "Don't tell me she's yours."

"I'm not!" Tricia said angrily.

The girl and I looked at each other. She could have been any of the hundred in the Green that afternoon—animated, poised, pretty in a robust way. "Maureen's at the College of Art," Michael said to me, and to her, "Ann's from America."

"When all's said and done," I said.

"Is it ever?" he asked.

"Sooner or later," I said.

The girl was impassive as if having got the drift of the conversation she knew she was its beneficiary and had only to wait it out.

"In Ireland," Michael said, "we've always a few last words on any subject."

"A few hundred, but all you need is one." My heart was thudding. My voice was none too steady. I said, "This child's ravenous. Goodbye, Michael." And I abruptly turned away.

"What's ravenous?" Tricia asked.

"Hungry."

"But I'm not hungry, I'm thirsty!"

"Oh Tricia, be still!" I said, and she began to cry. I took her hand, and we started across the street.

"You don't like me!" she sobbed out.

"Don't be silly."

When we reached the other side, she dropped my hand and stopped crying. "I'm not silly!" she said proudly.

Three or four doors down Grafton Street was the Aer Lingus office, and when we came to it, I said, "I have to go in here." It was a spur of the moment decision, and as soon as we were inside, I wanted to turn around and walk back out, but the young man behind the counter had looked up and was waiting for us to approach. I went and asked about the summer flight schedule to New York, and he reached for a brochure.

"Are you emigrating?" he said. I started to laugh as I told him I was American; then I started crying. He wasn't in the least disconcerted. Mistaken the Irish might be, but never apologetic and seldom at a loss for words. "You look Irish," he told me.

I blew my nose and said, "Do I?"

"A bit anyway," he said on second thought. "Maybe around the eyes."

Tricia began pulling on my hand. "When are we going to have tea?" she asked.

I said, "First I have to talk to this man."

"But why?"

"Because I'm thinking of going home."

After the incident at the rectory I considered skipping Sunday Mass but when I thought about it I resented having what amounted to a kind of dispossession forced on me— your past may not suit you in every respect but it's irreplaceable, and the Catholic tradition was what I belonged to. Though the brand I'd been given was all pious misconception, the Church told hard truths that recent experience had borne in on me. The implication of people in one another's lives, the moral tension that will develop out of the simplest circumstances, the pitfalls opened up by desire—I wasn't willing to repudiate all that simply because of irresponsible behavior on someone else's part, troubling though that behavior still was.

I solved the dilemma by hearing Mass at a series of different churches—the Carmelites' off Grafton Street, the University Church on Stephen's Green, the Pro-Cathedral—but they all involved taking a bus or a long walk, either of which was a lot of trouble on Sunday morning, and after a few weeks of this I fell back on the local parish. A stout priest usually said the twelve-fifteen there, but finally of course Father Broderick came out on the altar one Sunday. For the first few minutes I had the feeling he was looking straight at me, though that would have been practically impossible—I was at the side and towards the rear. As I watched him moving back and forth on the altar I wondered how he felt. I hoped he'd found a satisfactory explanation for the episode with me, that the whole business wouldn't eat away at him, and I thought I found evidence of some such return to normal that morning in his sermon.

"In accordance with the bishop's recommendation," he said, "we're continuing our talks on the theological virtues with the virtue of hope. There are three kinds of people in whom one can best see hope operating: First of all are those without it, the men and women who think only of themselves and their human desires and whose capacity to concern themselves with the welfare of others has got caught up with worldly affairs."

I had listened to that text or one like it too often for it to engage my interest, and I was soon distracted. Attending Mass in Ireland was my own kind of certification. Among that crowd I could feel as Catholic, anyway, as the rest—pious old women, men with hangovers and men with a saintly air of detachment, solid-looking matrons, rosy-cheeked girls. Each of them had an exceptional look that reminded me of the rough finish and rich pigmentation that gave my earthenware dishes their odd beauty; but if everyone there looked original, I also felt that collectively they amounted to a matched set—a notion that made me smile to myself. Ten months in Ireland had taught me that the truth was the Irish are quarrelsome people, always at odds with each other. But they could afford to indulge their differences. Nothing they said or did could change the fact that they belonged together.

Looking around me that morning I had to or finally could admit that this also amounted to something not so desirable—a birthright unexamined makes for a false sense of security. Whereas in America it was hard to sustain the illusion that your particular heritage was unrivaled. Any such state of mind was constantly subjected to the need to accommodate, to accept, to make allowances till eventually you were rubbed smooth. I thought of the blandly unmistakable Boston or Philadelphia or Milwaukee faces that were in season now in Dublin. The blandness, the colorlessness represented wonderful patience somewhere along the line and wonderful courage. There was no getting away from that, nor from the one tremendous drawback inherent in racial definition acquired too early and accepted too readily: Fascinating as this island was to itself (and to me) it wasn't the whole world—not my world anyway; I wasn't limited to Ireland. I began trying to remember exactly how much money I had in the bank, whether there was enough to get me, before I went home, to Paris and back. Or if not Paris, at least London.

Twenty-two I didn't exactly blame Tony Shields for the changed circumstances of my life but I did associate the change with him and the night he'd come to supper in the box room. When he called towards the end of June, I made some excuse for not going to Mooney's with him. He said he was leaving for Cavan the following week and would spend the summer there; I never saw the inside of Mooney's and I never saw Tony again.

I did see Tomás O'Domhnaill before I left Ireland. We ran into each other on Merrion Row which is a few yards past the Shelbourne, and the sort of unexceptional scene that's the common backdrop of the dreams of Dublin I have now. I'm always racing along some short dull stretch of sidewalk, heading for an unspecified destination that I never seem to reach. These dream streets are mostly unpopulated. Places rarely offer resistance to entering the unconscious—it's people who make difficulties, as Tomás O'Domhnaill did whenever we'd met, the last time included. It was the middle of the morning, and I wouldn't have expected him to be at large. I said, "What are you doing here?" and he told me he was up on business. I said, "I meant out and about at this hour."

"Ireland's a free country, too, you know." He spoke with barely an echo of his old belligerence, though I doubt that its full force would have provoked me at that stage. In fact I started to laugh and really set him off. "America's not the only place you can come and go as you please. The rest of the world isn't all savages and slaves. We were a civilized people long before ever Columbus set foot in the Western Hemisphere." In this brief tirade I finally heard the envious note that my own envy had all along deafened me to the sound of, and not only in Tomás but in Daisy and Annabel, in Molly Corcoran, in Mrs. Philbin and Theresa, probably in Tony Shields, certainly in Aideen Fitzgerald, maybe even in Martin Brodie who was there with Tomás that morning.

I turned to him and said, "Still going off into the night?"

"Some day never to return." Martin avoided my eyes, and I wondered whether Tomás had told him why I'd stopped joining them on their rounds. The likelihood was that he'd kept the truth to himself—it was more of a reflection on him than on me—but Martin seemed restless standing there, and so was Tomás; so was I. We said goodbye, and they went on down Merrion Row, probably to Nesbitt's, and I went my own way which was probably on to Grafton Street.

This routine encounter with its faint note of routine misunderstanding was the memory my thoughts crystallized around the other day after I learned that Tomás was in New York. At first I rejected the idea of another such meeting and went so far as to tear up the telephone message and drop it in the wastebasket; then I started wondering how he'd strike me after such a stretch of time and I fished the slip out of the basket. Piecing it together, reconstructing the phone number, I seemed to recall once spending an evening at the Abbey Victoria Hotel. Was I in college at the time? Probably. And who was with me? A blind date—that much I felt sure of, but on his identity I drew a blank, and also on details of the lounge where we must have sat around having drinks and listening to piano music.

What happens to you on home ground is truest to your life, taken more readily for granted and thus quicker than the humdrumest aspects of life abroad to recede into the shadows of the mind. The very vividness of my Irish memories called them into question, suggesting that at their most instructive they represented only a brief digression from the substance of my life. But to admit that was to risk losing the small claim I felt I still had to the yellow mountains and gray villages; Cork and Galway and Dublin—the duck pond in the Green, the dirty swans on the Liffey, the Georgian Squares, the box room, tea at Bewley's, *poulet sauté Jammet*. The vision of all this rose up again, filling me with an awful longing to be part of it at whatever cost, and I reached for the phone.

The surge of conflicting emotions that I'm prey to now and call "homesickness for Ireland" bears no resemblance to the real thing as I knew it—a *malaise* that occasionally came over me when I lived in Dublin. Hearing an American song on the radio usually brought it on, or seeing an American movie—a revival of "Breakfast at Tiffany's," for one. I was dazed by that glossy image of New York. I'd got used to Dublin's watery light, its modest scale, and when I returned here I kept marvelling at how scintillating this city really is. I marvel still—walking past the *Beaux Arts* splendors of the east side where I live, crossing the Park at night in a taxi, sitting in my office with its view of Manhattan's shimmering glass towers.

I was standing at my window that afternoon when Tomás O'Domhnaill was shown into the office. "Well so, Ann," he said, and I turned.

"You've grown a beard!"

He fingered it, looking around him and saying, "This is a fine place you have."

Beards are so common these days that his served to bring him disturbingly up to date. The washable, light gray suit he wore served the same purpose, but that one-sided, triangular bulk—his wiry hair—tied in with my image of the old-fashioned figure who'd interested and intimidated me when we met in Cork. I asked, "What brings you to America?"

"I was moved last year to the Dublin office. They've sent me over to a conference on human rights." The Tomás I'd known wasn't concerned with rights or conferences, and I could hardly keep from smiling as I went and sat at my desk; he took the spare chair beside it. "What sort of work do you do now?" he asked.

"I'm an associate producer," I told him.

He said, "I'm impressed."

"Please," I said, "don't be." A Tomás toned down was to have been wished for, but mellowed might be going too far. "Do you like New York?" I had an agreeable sense of exertion, as if we were rowing towards each other, moving by means of these short, strenuous questions away from the shores of memory and out into the bright flux of the present.

"It's a bit loud here," said Tomás.

"A bit!" I said, and the familiar chip briefly appeared on his shoulder.

"There's noise round-the-clock—that's a fact. I didn't close an eye last night."

The Abbey Victoria is on Seventh Avenue, surrounded by bars and record stores and novelty shops going full blast all day and into the small hours. "Why did you pick that hotel?" I asked, and he grinned.

"In honor of Yeats, of course."

Perversity and pride, shrewdness and innocence. Inno-

cent Tomás indeed was of this city—as I'd once been of his.
But Dublin had left its mark, investing me with its own skepticism, instructing me in its artful ways. "How did you know
where to find me?" I asked.

He said, "Dublin's a small city."

"Oh, come on, don't give me that," I said, but he justified his use of the old ploy.

"I interviewed Oona Ross when she got elected to the
Academy. It came out that you're friends."

"Better friends now than when we lived a block apart,"
I said.

"Distance lends enchantment."

"And a change of scene works wonders." Oona comes
to this country regularly, to teach or to lecture. "When she's
in New York she stays with me," I said, "and I manage to
get her organized."

He looked past me, saying, "I thought sure you'd have
a husband by now."

Was it my imagination, or did I see our last box room
encounter flicker behind his eyes? At any rate it crossed my
own mind. I wondered whether what happened that night
had been, as much as anything else, a matter of my own cal-
lowness—for things not to get out of hand, you must first
appreciate the ease with which they can. I asked Tomás how
long he planned to be in New York; he told me a fortnight,
and echoes of the derision that used to greet my American-
isms made me object. "You mean two weeks."

"If you say so."

"We do." How much, if any, of his fortnight would he
want to spend with me, and how would his company strike
me now? He looked exceedingly rough-hewn, the Dacron suit
notwithstanding, and I've come to admire the polished look
of people here. I couldn't quite picture Tomás at the pretty
neighborhood restaurants where I meet my friends, at dinner in their comfortable apartments, at my family's rented
beach house, with Barbara and the erudite man she has married.

"Will we have a drink somewhere, Ann?"

I hesitated. But Tomás O'Domhnaill was the source of my strongest impressions of Dublin and of some of the liveliest hours I'd spent there. With his rude energy and rough common sense he epitomized the city and all that I cherished it for. He had, after a fashion, taken me under his wing there, and in return I would take him, in some fashion, under mine. "We will," I said.

Carnegie Public Library
Two Harbors, Minnesota 55616

RULES

1. Books may be kept two weeks and may be renewed once for the same period, except 7 day books and magazines.

2. A fine is charged for each day a book is not returned, according to the above rule. No book will be issued to any person incurring such a fine until it has been paid.

3. All injuries to books beyond reasonable wear and all losses shall be made good to the satisfaction of the Librarian.

4. Each borrower is held responsible for all books drawn on his card and for all fines accruing on the same.

DEMCO